**Henry James** OM (15 April 1843 – 28 February 1916) was an American-British author regarded as a key transitional figure between literary realism and literary modernism, and is considered by many to be among the greatest novelists in the English language. He was the son of Henry James Sr. and the brother of renowned philosopher and psychologist William James and diarist Alice James.

He is best known for a number of novels dealing with the social and marital interplay between émigré Americans, English people, and continental Europeans. Examples of such novels include The Portrait of a Lady, The Ambassadors, and The Wings of the Dove. His later works were increasingly experimental. In describing the internal states of mind and social dynamics of his characters, James often made use of a style in which ambiguous or contradictory motives and impressions were overlaid or juxtaposed in the discussion of a character's psyche.(Source: Wikipedia)

**Literary works:**
Watch and Ward (1871)
Roderick Hudson (1875)
The American (1877)
The Europeans (1878)
Confidence (1879)
Washington Square (1880)
The Portrait of a Lady (1881)
The Bostonians (1886)
The Princess Casamassima (1886)
The Reverberator (1888)
The Tragic Muse (1890)
The Other House (1896)
The Spoils of Poynton (1897)
What Maisie Knew (1897)

PRINCE CLASSICS

# PANDORA

## HENRY JAMES

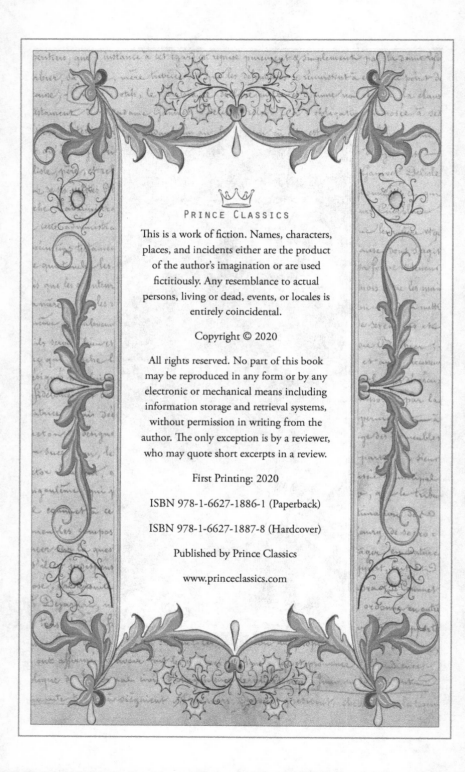

## PRINCE CLASSICS

First Printing: 2020

ISBN 978-1-6627-1886-1 (Paperback)

ISBN 978-1-6627-1887-8 (Hardcover)

Published by Prince Classics

www.princeclassics.com

# Contents

# PANDORA

# I

It has long been the custom of the North German Lloyd steamers, which convey passengers from Bremen to New York, to anchor for several hours in the pleasant port of Southampton, where their human cargo receives many additions. An intelligent young German, Count Otto Vogelstein, hardly knew a few years ago whether to condemn this custom or approve it. He leaned over the bulwarks of the *Donau* as the American passengers crossed the plank—the travellers who embark at Southampton are mainly of that nationality—and curiously, indifferently, vaguely, through the smoke of his cigar, saw them absorbed in the huge capacity of the ship, where he had the agreeable consciousness that his own nest was comfortably made. To watch from such a point of vantage the struggles of those less fortunate than ourselves—of the uninformed, the unprovided, the belated, the bewildered—is an occupation not devoid of sweetness, and there was nothing to mitigate the complacency with which our young friend gave himself up to it; nothing, that is, save a natural benevolence which had not yet been extinguished by the consciousness of official greatness. For Count Vogelstein was official, as I think you would have seen from the straightness of his back, the lustre of his light elegant spectacles, and something discreet and diplomatic in the curve of his moustache, which looked as if it might well contribute to the principal function, as cynics say, of the lips—the active concealment of thought. He had been appointed to the secretaryship of the German legation at Washington and in these first days of the autumn was about to take possession of his post. He was a model character for such a purpose—serious civil ceremonious curious stiff, stuffed with knowledge and convinced that, as lately rearranged, the German Empire places in the most striking light the highest of all the possibilities of the greatest of all the peoples. He was quite aware, however, of the claims to economic and other consideration of the United States, and that this quarter of the globe offered a vast field for study.

The process of inquiry had already begun for him, in spite of his having as yet spoken to none of his fellow-passengers; the case being that

Vogelstein inquired not only with his tongue, but with his eyes—that is with his spectacles—with his ears, with his nose, with his palate, with all his senses and organs. He was a highly upright young man, whose only fault was that his sense of comedy, or of the humour of things, had never been specifically disengaged from his several other senses. He vaguely felt that something should be done about this, and in a general manner proposed to do it, for he was on his way to explore a society abounding in comic aspects. This consciousness of a missing measure gave him a certain mistrust of what might be said of him; and if circumspection is the essence of diplomacy our young aspirant promised well. His mind contained several millions of facts, packed too closely together for the light breeze of the imagination to draw through the mass. He was impatient to report himself to his superior in Washington, and the loss of time in an English port could only incommode him, inasmuch as the study of English institutions was no part of his mission. On the other hand the day was charming; the blue sea, in Southampton Water, pricked all over with light, had no movement but that of its infinite shimmer. Moreover he was by no means sure that he should be happy in the United States, where doubtless he should find himself soon enough disembarked. He knew that this was not an important question and that happiness was an unscientific term, such as a man of his education should be ashamed to use even in the silence of his thoughts. Lost none the less in the inconsiderate crowd and feeling himself neither in his own country nor in that to which he was in a manner accredited, he was reduced to his mere personality; so that during the hour, to save his importance, he cultivated such ground as lay in sight for a judgement of this delay to which the German steamer was subjected in English waters. Mightn't it be proved, facts, figures and documents—or at least watch—in hand, considerably greater than the occasion demanded?

Count Vogelstein was still young enough in diplomacy to think it necessary to have opinions. He had a good many indeed which had been formed without difficulty; they had been received ready-made from a line of ancestors who knew what they liked. This was of course—and under pressure, being candid, he would have admitted it—an unscientific way of furnishing one's mind. Our young man was a stiff conservative, a Junker of Junkers; he thought modern democracy a temporary phase and expected to find many arguments against it in the great Republic. In regard to these things it was a pleasure to him to feel that, with his complete training, he had been taught thoroughly to appreciate the nature of evidence. The ship was heavily laden with German emigrants, whose mission in the United States differed considerably from Count Otto's. They hung over the bulwarks, densely grouped; they leaned forward on their elbows for hours, their shoulders kept on a level with their ears; the men in furred caps, smoking long-bowled pipes, the women with babies hidden in remarkably ugly shawls. Some were yellow Germans and some were black, and all looked greasy and matted with the sea-damp. They were destined to swell still further the huge current of the Western democracy; and Count Vogelstein doubtless said to himself that they wouldn't improve its quality. Their numbers, however, were striking, and I know not what he thought of the nature of this particular evidence.

The passengers who came on board at Southampton were not of the greasy class; they were for the most part American families who had been spending the summer, or a longer period, in Europe. They had a great deal of luggage, innumerable bags and rugs and hampers and sea-chairs, and were composed largely of ladies of various ages, a little pale with anticipation, wrapped also in striped shawls, though in prettier ones than the nursing mothers of the steerage, and crowned with very high hats and feathers. They darted to and fro across the gangway, looking for each other and for their scattered parcels; they separated and reunited, they exclaimed and declared, they eyed with dismay the occupants of the forward quarter, who seemed numerous enough to sink the vessel, and their voices sounded faint and far as they rose to Vogelstein's ear over the latter's great tarred sides. He noticed that in the new contingent there were many young girls, and he remembered what a lady in Dresden had once said to him—that America was the country of the Mädchen. He wondered whether he should like that, and reflected that it would be an aspect to study, like everything else. He had known in Dresden an American family in which there were three daughters who used to skate with the officers, and some of the ladies now coming on board struck him as of that same habit, except that in the Dresden days feathers weren't worn quite so high.

At last the ship began to creak and slowly bridge, and the delay at Southampton came to an end. The gangway was removed and the vessel indulged in the awkward evolutions that were to detach her from the land. Count Vogelstein had finished his cigar, and he spent a long time in walking up and down the upper deck. The charming English coast passed before him, and he felt this to be the last of the old world. The American coast also might be pretty—he hardly knew what one would expect of an American coast; but he was sure it would be different. Differences, however, were notoriously half the charm of travel, and perhaps even most when they couldn't be expressed in figures, numbers, diagrams or the other merely useful symbols. As yet indeed there were very few among the objects presented to sight on the steamer. Most of his fellow-passengers appeared of one and the same persuasion, and that persuasion the least to be mistaken. They were Jews and commercial to a man. And by this time they had lighted their cigars and put on all manner of seafaring caps, some of them with big ear-lappets which somehow had the effect of bringing out their peculiar facial type. At last the new voyagers began to emerge from below and to look about them, vaguely, with that suspicious expression of face always to be noted in the newly embarked and which, as directed to the receding land, resembles that of a person who begins to perceive himself the victim of a trick. Earth and ocean, in such glances, are made the subject of a sweeping objection, and many travellers, in the general plight, have an air at once duped and superior, which seems to say that they could easily go ashore if they would.

It still wanted two hours of dinner, and by the time Vogelstein's long legs had measured three or four miles on the deck he was ready to settle himself in his sea-chair and draw from his pocket a Tauchnitz novel by an American author whose pages, he had been assured, would help to prepare him for some of the oddities. On the back of his chair his name was painted in rather large letters, this being a precaution taken at the recommendation of a friend who had told him that on the American steamers the passengers—especially the ladies—thought nothing of pilfering one's little comforts. His friend had even hinted at the correct reproduction of his coronet. This marked man of the world had added that the Americans are greatly impressed by a coronet. I know not whether it was scepticism or modesty, but Count

Vogelstein had omitted every pictured plea for his rank; there were others of which he might have made use. The precious piece of furniture which on the Atlantic voyage is trusted never to flinch among universal concussions was emblazoned simply with his title and name. It happened, however, that the blazonry was huge; the back of the chair was covered with enormous German characters. This time there can be no doubt: it was modesty that caused the secretary of legation, in placing himself, to turn this portion of his seat outward, away from the eyes of his companions—to present it to the balustrade of the deck. The ship was passing the Needles—the beautiful uttermost point of the Isle of Wight. Certain tall white cones of rock rose out of the purple sea; they flushed in the afternoon light and their vague rosiness gave them a human expression in face of the cold expanse toward which the prow was turned; they seemed to say farewell, to be the last note of a peopled world. Vogelstein saw them very comfortably from his place and after a while turned his eyes to the other quarter, where the elements of air and water managed to make between them so comparatively poor an opposition. Even his American novelist was more amusing than that, and he prepared to return to this author. In the great curve which it described, however, his glance was arrested by the figure of a young lady who had just ascended to the deck and who paused at the mouth of the companionway.

This was not in itself an extraordinary phenomenon; but what attracted Vogelstein's attention was the fact that the young person appeared to have fixed her eyes on him. She was slim, brightly dressed, rather pretty; Vogelstein remembered in a moment that he had noticed her among the people on the wharf at Southampton. She was soon aware he had observed her; whereupon she began to move along the deck with a step that seemed to indicate a purpose of approaching him. Vogelstein had time to wonder whether she could be one of the girls he had known at Dresden; but he presently reflected that they would now be much older than that. It was true they were apt to advance, like this one, straight upon their victim. Yet the present specimen was no longer looking at him, and though she passed near him it was now tolerably clear she had come above but to take a general survey. She was a quick handsome competent girl, and she simply wanted to see what one could think of the ship, of the weather, of the appearance of England, from

13

such a position as that; possibly even of one's fellow-passengers. She satisfied herself promptly on these points, and then she looked about, while she walked, as if in keen search of a missing object; so that Vogelstein finally arrived at a conviction of her real motive. She passed near him again and this time almost stopped, her eyes bent upon him attentively. He thought her conduct remarkable even after he had gathered that it was not at his face, with its yellow moustache, she was looking, but at the chair on which he was seated. Then those words of his friend came back to him—the speech about the tendency of the people, especially of the ladies, on the American steamers to take to themselves one's little belongings. Especially the ladies, he might well say; for here was one who apparently wished to pull from under him the very chair he was sitting on. He was afraid she would ask him for it, so he pretended to read, systematically avoiding her eye. He was conscious she hovered near him, and was moreover curious to see what she would do. It seemed to him strange that such a nice-looking girl—for her appearance was really charming—should endeavour by arts so flagrant to work upon the quiet dignity of a secretary of legation. At last it stood out that she was trying to look round a corner, as it were—trying to see what was written on the back of his chair. "She wants to find out my name; she wants to see who I am!" This reflexion passed through his mind and caused him to raise his eyes. They rested on her own—which for an appreciable moment she didn't withdraw. The latter were brilliant and expressive, and surmounted a delicate aquiline nose, which, though pretty, was perhaps just a trifle too hawk-like. It was the oddest coincidence in the world; the story Vogelstein had taken up treated of a flighty forward little American girl who plants herself in front of a young man in the garden of an hotel. Wasn't the conduct of this young lady a testimony to the truthfulness of the tale, and wasn't Vogelstein himself in the position of the young man in the garden? That young man—though with more, in such connexions in general, to go upon—ended by addressing himself to his aggressor, as she might be called, and after a very short hesitation Vogelstein followed his example. "If she wants to know who I am she's welcome," he said to himself; and he got out of the chair, seized it by the back and, turning it round, exhibited the superscription to the girl. She coloured slightly, but smiled and read his name, while Vogelstein raised his hat.

"I'm much obliged to you. That's all right," she remarked as if the discovery had made her very happy.

It affected him indeed as all right that he should be Count Otto Vogelstein; this appeared even rather a flippant mode of disposing of the fact. By way of rejoinder he asked her if she desired of him the surrender of his seat.

"I'm much obliged to you; of course not. I thought you had one of our chairs, and I didn't like to ask you. It looks exactly like one of ours; not so much now as when you sit in it. Please sit down again. I don't want to trouble you. We've lost one of ours, and I've been looking for it everywhere. They look so much alike; you can't tell till you see the back. Of course I see there will be no mistake about yours," the young lady went on with a smile of which the serenity matched her other abundance. "But we've got such a small name—you can scarcely see it," she added with the same friendly intention. "Our name's just Day—you mightn't think it *was* a name, might you? if we didn't make the most of it. If you see that on anything, I'd be so obliged if you'd tell me. It isn't for myself, it's for my mother; she's so dependent on her chair, and that one I'm looking for pulls out so beautifully. Now that you sit down again and hide the lower part it does look just like ours. Well, it must be somewhere. You must excuse me; I wouldn't disturb you."

This was a long and even confidential speech for a young woman, presumably unmarried, to make to a perfect stranger; but Miss Day acquitted herself of it with perfect simplicity and self-possession. She held up her head and stepped away, and Vogelstein could see that the foot she pressed upon the clean smooth deck was slender and shapely. He watched her disappear through the trap by which she had ascended, and he felt more than ever like the young man in his American tale. The girl in the present case was older and not so pretty, as he could easily judge, for the image of her smiling eyes and speaking lips still hovered before him. He went back to his book with the feeling that it would give him some information about her. This was rather illogical, but it indicated a certain amount of curiosity on the part of Count Vogelstein. The girl in the book had a mother, it appeared, and so had this young lady; the former had also a brother, and he now remembered that he had noticed a young man on the wharf—a young man in a high hat and a white overcoat—who seemed united to Miss Day by this natural tie. And there was some one else too, as he gradually recollected, an older man, also in a high hat, but in a black overcoat—in black altogether—who completed the group and who was presumably the head of the family. These reflexions would indicate that Count Vogelstein read his volume of Tauchnitz rather interruptedly. Moreover they represented but the loosest economy of consciousness; for wasn't he to be afloat in an oblong box for ten days with such people, and could it be doubted he should see at least enough of them?

It may as well be written without delay that he saw a great deal of them. I have sketched in some detail the conditions in which he made the acquaintance of Miss Day, because the event had a certain importance for this fair square Teuton; but I must pass briefly over the incidents that immediately followed it. He wondered what it was open to him, after such an introduction, to do in relation to her, and he determined he would push through his American tale and discover what the hero did. But he satisfied himself in a very short time that Miss Day had nothing in common with the heroine of that work save certain signs of habitat and climate—and save, further, the fact that the male sex wasn't terrible to her. The local stamp sharply, as he gathered, impressed upon her he estimated indeed rather in a borrowed than in a natural light, for if she was native to a small town in the interior of the American continent one of their fellow-passengers, a lady from New York with whom he had a good deal of conversation, pronounced her "atrociously" provincial. How the lady arrived at this certitude didn't appear, for Vogelstein observed that she held no communication with the girl. It was true she gave it the support of her laying down that certain Americans could tell immediately who other Americans were, leaving him to judge whether or no she herself belonged to the critical or only to the criticised half of the nation. Mrs. Dangerfield was a handsome confidential insinuating woman, with whom Vogelstein felt his talk take a very wide range indeed. She convinced him rather effectually that even in a great democracy there are human differences, and that American life was full of social distinctions, of delicate shades, which foreigners often lack the intelligence to perceive. Did he suppose every one knew every one else in the biggest country in the world, and that one wasn't as free to choose one's company there as in the most monarchical and most exclusive societies? She laughed such delusions to scorn as Vogelstein tucked her beautiful furred coverlet—they reclined together a great deal in their elongated chairs—well over her feet. How free an American lady was to choose her company she abundantly proved by not knowing any one on the steamer but Count Otto.

He could see for himself that Mr. and Mrs. Day had not at all her grand air. They were fat plain serious people who sat side by side on the deck for hours and looked straight before them. Mrs. Day had a white face, large cheeks and small eyes: her forehead was surrounded with a multitude of little tight black curls; her lips moved as if she had always a lozenge in her mouth. She wore entwined about her head an article which Mrs. Dangerfield spoke of as a "nuby," a knitted pink scarf concealing her hair, encircling her neck and having among its convolutions a hole for her perfectly expressionless face. Her hands were folded on her stomach, and in her still, swathed figure her little bead-like eyes, which occasionally changed their direction, alone represented life. Her husband had a stiff grey beard on his chin and a bare spacious upper lip, to which constant shaving had imparted a hard glaze. His eyebrows were thick and his nostrils wide, and when he was uncovered, in the saloon, it was visible that his grizzled hair was dense and perpendicular. He might have looked rather grim and truculent hadn't it been for the mild familiar accommodating gaze with which his large light-coloured pupils— the leisurely eyes of a silent man—appeared to consider surrounding objects. He was evidently more friendly than fierce, but he was more diffident than friendly. He liked to have you in sight, but wouldn't have pretended to understand you much or to classify you, and would have been sorry it should put you under an obligation. He and his wife spoke sometimes, but seldom talked, and there was something vague and patient in them, as if they had become victims of a wrought spell. The spell however was of no sinister cast; it was the fascination of prosperity, the confidence of security, which sometimes makes people arrogant, but which had had such a different effect on this simple satisfied pair, in whom further development of every kind appeared to have been happily arrested.

Mrs. Dangerfield made it known to Count Otto that every morning after breakfast, the hour at which he wrote his journal in his cabin, the

17

old couple were guided upstairs and installed in their customary corner by Pandora. This she had learned to be the name of their elder daughter, and she was immensely amused by her discovery. "Pandora"—that was in the highest degree typical; it placed them in the social scale if other evidence had been wanting; you could tell that a girl was from the interior, the mysterious interior about which Vogelstein's imagination was now quite excited, when she had such a name as that. This young lady managed the whole family, even a little the small beflounced sister, who, with bold pretty innocent eyes, a torrent of fair silky hair, a crimson fez, such as is worn by male Turks, very much askew on top of it, and a way of galloping and straddling about the ship in any company she could pick up—she had long thin legs, very short skirts and stockings of every tint—was going home, in elegant French clothes, to resume an interrupted education. Pandora overlooked and directed her relatives; Vogelstein could see this for himself, could see she was very active and decided, that she had in a high degree the sentiment of responsibility, settling on the spot most of the questions that could come up for a family from the interior.

The voyage was remarkably fine, and day after day it was possible to sit there under the salt sky and feel one's self rounding the great curves of the globe. The long deck made a white spot in the sharp black circle of the ocean and in the intense sea-light, while the shadow of the smoke-streamers trembled on the familiar floor, the shoes of fellow-passengers, distinctive now, and in some cases irritating, passed and repassed, accompanied, in the air so tremendously "open," that rendered all voices weak and most remarks rather flat, by fragments of opinion on the run of the ship. Vogelstein by this time had finished his little American story and now definitely judged that Pandora Day was not at all like the heroine. She was of quite another type; much more serious and strenuous, and not at all keen, as he had supposed, about making the acquaintance of gentlemen. Her speaking to him that first afternoon had been, he was bound to believe, an incident without importance for herself; in spite of her having followed it up the next day by the remark, thrown at him as she passed, with a smile that was almost fraternal: "It's all right, sir! I've found that old chair." After this she hadn't spoken to him again and had scarcely looked at him. She read a great deal, and almost always French books, in fresh yellow paper; not the lighter forms of that literature, but a volume of Sainte-Beuve, of Renan or at the most, in the way of dissipation, of Alfred de Musset. She took frequent exercise and almost always walked alone, apparently not having made many friends on the ship and being without the resource of her parents, who, as has been related, never budged out of the cosy corner in which she planted them for the day.

Her brother was always in the smoking-room, where Vogelstein observed him, in very tight clothes, his neck encircled with a collar like a palisade. He had a sharp little face, which was not disagreeable; he smoked enormous cigars and began his drinking early in the day: but his appearance gave no sign of these excesses. As regards euchre and poker and the other distractions of the place he was guilty of none. He evidently understood such games in perfection, for he used to watch the players, and even at moments impartially advise them; but Vogelstein never saw the cards in his hand. He was referred to as regards disputed points, and his opinion carried the day. He took little part in the conversation, usually much relaxed, that prevailed in the smoking-room, but from time to time he made, in his soft flat youthful voice, a remark which every one paused to listen to and which was greeted with roars of laughter. Vogelstein, well as he knew English, could rarely catch the joke; but he could see at least that these must be choice specimens of that American humour admired and practised by a whole continent and yet to be rendered accessible to a trained diplomatist, clearly, but by some special and incalculable revelation. The young man, in his way, was very remarkable, for, as Vogelstein heard some one say once after the laughter had subsided, he was only nineteen. If his sister didn't resemble the dreadful little girl in the tale already mentioned, there was for Vogelstein at least an analogy between young Mr. Day and a certain small brother—a candy-loving Madison, Hamilton or Jefferson—who was, in the Tauchnitz volume, attributed to that unfortunate maid. This was what the little Madison would have grown up to at nineteen, and the improvement was greater than might have been expected.

The days were long, but the voyage was short, and it had almost come to an end before Count Otto yielded to an attraction peculiar in its nature and finally irresistible, and, in spite of Mrs. Dangerfield's emphatic warning, sought occasion for a little continuous talk with Miss Pandora. To mention that this impulse took effect without mentioning sundry other of his current impressions with which it had nothing to do is perhaps to violate proportion and give a false idea; but to pass it by would be still more unjust. The Germans, as we know, are a transcendental people, and there was at last an irresistible appeal for Vogelstein in this quick bright silent girl who could smile and turn vocal in an instant, who imparted a rare originality to the filial character, and whose profile was delicate as she bent it over a volume which she cut as she read, or presented it in musing attitudes, at the side of the ship, to the horizon they had left behind. But he felt it to be a pity, as regards a possible acquaintance with her, that her parents should be heavy little burghers, that her brother should not correspond to his conception of a young man of the upper class, and that her sister should be a Daisy Miller *en herbe*. Repeatedly admonished by Mrs. Dangerfield, the young diplomatist was doubly careful as to the relations he might form at the beginning of his sojourn in the United States. That lady reminded him, and he had himself made the observation in other capitals, that the first year, and even the second, is the time for prudence. One was ignorant of proportions and values; one was exposed to mistakes and thankful for attention, and one might give one's self away to people who would afterwards be as a millstone round one's neck: Mrs. Dangerfield struck and sustained that note, which resounded in the young man's imagination. She assured him that if he didn't "look out" he would be committing himself to some American girl with an impossible family. In America, when one committed one's self, there was nothing to do but march to the altar, and what should he say for instance to finding himself a near relation of Mr. and Mrs. P. W. Day?—since such were the initials inscribed on the back of the two chairs of that couple. Count Otto felt the peril, for he could immediately think of a dozen men he knew who had married American girls. There appeared now to be a constant danger of marrying the American girl; it was something one had to reckon with, like the railway, the telegraph, the discovery of dynamite, the Chassepôt rifle, the Socialistic spirit: it was one of the complications of modern life.

It would doubtless be too much to say that he feared being carried away by a passion for a young woman who was not strikingly beautiful and with whom he had talked, in all, but ten minutes. But, as we recognise, he went so far as to wish that the human belongings of a person whose high spirit appeared to have no taint either of fastness, as they said in England, or of subversive opinion, and whose mouth had charming lines, should not be a little more distinguished. There was an effect of drollery in her behaviour to these subjects of her zeal, whom she seemed to regard as a care, but not as an interest; it was as if they had been entrusted to her honour and she had engaged to convey them safe to a certain point; she was detached and inadvertent, and then suddenly remembered, repented and came back to tuck them into their blankets, to alter the position of her mother's umbrella, to tell them something about the run of the ship. These little offices were usually performed deftly, rapidly, with the minimum of words, and when their daughter drew near them Mr. and Mrs. Day closed their eyes after the fashion of a pair of household dogs who expect to be scratched.

One morning she brought up the Captain of the ship to present to them; she appeared to have a private and independent acquaintance with this officer, and the introduction to her parents had the air of a sudden happy thought. It wasn't so much an introduction as an exhibition, as if she were saying to him: "This is what they look like; see how comfortable I make them. Aren't they rather queer and rather dear little people? But they leave me perfectly free. Oh I can assure you of that. Besides, you must see it for yourself." Mr. and Mrs. Day looked up at the high functionary who thus unbent to them with very little change of countenance; then looked at each other in the same way. He saluted, he inclined himself a moment; but Pandora shook her head, she seemed to be answering for them; she made little gestures as if in explanation to the good Captain of some of their peculiarities, as for instance that he needn't expect them to speak. They closed their eyes at last; she appeared to have a kind of mesmeric influence on them, and Miss Day walked away with the important friend, who treated her with evident consideration, bowing very low, for all his importance, when the two presently after separated. Vogelstein could see she was capable of making an impression; and the moral of our little matter is that in spite of Mrs. Dangerfield, in spite of the resolutions of his prudence, in spite of the limits of such acquaintance as he had momentarily made with her, in spite of Mr. and Mrs. Day and the young man in the smoking-room, she had fixed his attention.

It was in the course of the evening after the scene with the Captain that he joined her, awkwardly, abruptly, irresistibly, on the deck, where she was pacing to and fro alone, the hour being auspiciously mild and the stars remarkably fine. There were scattered talkers and smokers and couples, unrecognisable, that moved quickly through the gloom. The vessel dipped with long regular pulsations; vague and spectral under the low stars, its swaying pinnacles spotted here and there with lights, it seemed to rush through the darkness faster than by day. Count Otto had come up to walk, and as the girl brushed past him he distinguished Pandora's face—with Mrs. Dangerfield he always spoke of her as Pandora—under the veil worn to protect it from the sea-damp. He stopped, turned, hurried after her, threw away his cigar—then asked her if she would do him the honour to accept his arm. She declined his arm but accepted his company, and he allowed her to enjoy it for an hour. They had a great deal of talk, and he was to remember afterwards some of the things she had said. There was now a certainty of the ship's getting into dock the next morning but one, and this prospect afforded an obvious topic. Some of Miss Day's expressions struck him as singular, but of course, as he was aware, his knowledge of English was not nice enough to give him a perfect measure.

"I'm not in a hurry to arrive; I'm very happy here," she said. "I'm afraid I shall have such a time putting my people through."

"Putting them through?"

"Through the Custom-House. We've made so many purchases. Well, I've written to a friend to come down, and perhaps he can help us. He's very well acquainted with the head. Once I'm chalked I don't care. I feel like a kind of blackboard by this time anyway. We found them awful in Germany."

Count Otto wondered if the friend she had written to were her lover and if they had plighted their troth, especially when she alluded to him again as "that gentleman who's coming down." He asked her about her travels, her impressions, whether she had been long in Europe and what she liked best, and she put it to him that they had gone abroad, she and her family, for a little fresh experience. Though he found her very intelligent he suspected she gave this as a reason because he was a German and she had heard the Germans were rich in culture. He wondered what form of culture Mr. and Mrs. Day had brought back from Italy, Greece and Palestine—they had travelled for two years and been everywhere—especially when their daughter said: "I wanted father and mother to see the best things. I kept them three hours on the Acropolis. I guess they won't forget that!" Perhaps it was of Phidias and Pericles they were thinking, Vogelstein reflected, as they sat ruminating in their rugs. Pandora remarked also that she wanted to show her little sister everything while she was comparatively unformed ("comparatively!" he mutely gasped); remarkable sights made so much more impression when the mind was fresh: she had read something of that sort somewhere in Goethe. She had wanted to come herself when she was her sister's age; but her father was in business then and they couldn't leave Utica. The young man thought of the little sister frisking over the Parthenon and the Mount of Olives and sharing for two years, the years of the school-room, this extraordinary pilgrimage of her parents; he wondered whether Goethe's dictum had been justified in this case. He asked Pandora if Utica were the seat of her family, if it were an important or typical place, if it would be an interesting city for him, as a stranger, to see. His companion replied frankly that this was a big question, but added that all the same she would ask him to "come and visit us at our home" if it weren't that they should probably soon leave it.

"Ah, you're going to live elsewhere?" Vogelstein asked, as if that fact too would be typical.

"Well, I'm working for New York. I flatter myself I've loosened them while we've been away," the girl went on. "They won't find in Utica the same charm; that was my idea. I want a big place, and of course Utica—!" She broke off as before a complex statement.

"I suppose Utica is inferior—?" Vogelstein seemed to see his way to suggest.

"Well no, I guess I can't have you call Utica inferior. It isn't supreme—that's what's the matter with it, and I hate anything middling," said Pandora Day. She gave a light dry laugh, tossing back her head a little as she made this declaration. And looking at her askance in the dusk, as she trod the deck that vaguely swayed, he recognised something in her air and port that matched such a pronouncement.

"What's her social position?" he inquired of Mrs. Dangerfield the next day. "I can't make it out at all—it's so contradictory. She strikes me as having much cultivation and much spirit. Her appearance, too, is very neat. Yet her parents are complete little burghers. That's easily seen."

"Oh, social position," and Mrs. Dangerfield nodded two or three times portentously. "What big expressions you use! Do you think everybody in the world has a social position? That's reserved for an infinitely small majority of mankind. You can't have a social position at Utica any more than you can have an opera-box. Pandora hasn't got one; where, if you please, should she have got it? Poor girl, it isn't fair of you to make her the subject of such questions as that."

"Well," said Vogelstein, "if she's of the lower class it seems to me very—very—" And he paused a moment, as he often paused in speaking English, looking for his word.

"Very what, dear Count?"

"Very significant, very representative."

"Oh dear, she isn't of the lower class," Mrs. Dangerfield returned with an irritated sense of wasted wisdom. She liked to explain her country, but that somehow always required two persons.

"What is she then?"

"Well, I'm bound to admit that since I was at home last she's a novelty. A girl like that with such people—it *is* a new type."

"I like novelties"—and Count Otto smiled with an air of considerable resolution. He couldn't however be satisfied with a demonstration that only begged the question; and when they disembarked in New York he felt, even amid the confusion of the wharf and the heaps of disembowelled baggage, a certain acuteness of regret at the idea that Pandora and her family were about to vanish into the unknown. He had a consolation however: it was apparent that for some reason or other—illness or absence from town—the gentleman to whom she had written had not, as she said, come down. Vogelstein was glad—he couldn't have told you why—that this sympathetic person had failed her; even though without him Pandora had to engage single-handed with the United States Custom-House. Our young man's first impression of the Western world was received on the landing-place of the German steamers at Jersey City—a huge wooden shed covering a wooden wharf which resounded under the feet, an expanse palisaded with rough-hewn piles that leaned this way and that, and bestrewn with masses of heterogeneous luggage. At one end; toward the town, was a row of tall painted palings, behind which he could distinguish a press of hackney-coachmen, who brandished their whips and awaited their victims, while their voices rose, incessant, with a sharp strange sound, a challenge at once fierce and familiar. The whole place, behind the fence, appeared to bristle and resound. Out there was America, Count Otto said to himself, and he looked toward it with a sense that he should have to muster resolution. On the wharf people were rushing about amid their trunks, pulling their things together, trying to unite their scattered parcels. They were heated and angry, or else quite bewildered and discouraged. The few that had succeeded in collecting their battered boxes had an air of flushed indifference to the efforts of their neighbours, not even looking at people with whom they had been fondly intimate on the steamer. A detachment of the officers of the Customs was in attendance, and energetic passengers were engaged in attempts to drag them toward their luggage or to drag heavy pieces toward them. These functionaries were good-natured and taciturn, except when occasionally they remarked to a passenger whose open trunk stared up at them, eloquent, imploring, that they were afraid the voyage had been "rather glassy." They had a friendly leisurely speculative way of discharging their duty, and if they perceived a victim's name written on the portmanteau they addressed him by it in a tone of old acquaintance. Vogelstein found however that if they were familiar they weren't indiscreet. He had heard that in America all public functionaries were the same, that there wasn't a different *tenue*, as they said in France, for different positions, and he wondered whether at Washington the President and ministers, whom he expected to see—to *have* to see—a good deal of, would be like that.

He was diverted from these speculations by the sight of Mr. and Mrs. Day seated side by side upon a trunk and encompassed apparently by the accumulations of their tour. Their faces expressed more consciousness of surrounding objects than he had hitherto recognised, and there was an air of placid expansion in the mysterious couple which suggested that this consciousness was agreeable. Mr. and Mrs. Day were, as they would have said, real glad to get back. At a little distance, on the edge of the dock, our observer remarked their son, who had found a place where, between the sides of two big ships, he could see the ferry-boats pass; the large pyramidal low-laden ferry-boats of American waters. He stood there, patient and considering, with his small neat foot on a coil of rope, his back to everything that had been disembarked, his neck elongated in its polished cylinder, while the fragrance of his big cigar mingled with the odour of the rotting piles, and his little sister, beside him, hugged a huge post and tried to see how far she could crane over the water without falling in. Vogelstein's servant was off in search of an examiner; Count Otto himself had got his things together and was waiting to be released, fully expecting that for a person of his importance the ceremony would be brief.

Before it began he said a word to young Mr. Day, raising his hat at the same time to the little girl, whom he had not yet greeted and who dodged his salute by swinging herself boldly outward to the dangerous side of the pier. She was indeed still unformed, but was evidently as light as a feather.

"I see you're kept waiting like me. It's very tiresome," Count Otto said.

The young American answered without looking behind him. "As soon as we're started we'll go all right. My sister has written to a gentleman to come down."

"I've looked for Miss Day to bid her good-bye," Vogelstein went on; "but I don't see her."

"I guess she has gone to meet that gentleman; he's a great friend of hers."

"I guess he's her lover!" the little girl broke out. "She was always writing to him in Europe."

Her brother puffed his cigar in silence a moment. "That was only for this. I'll tell on you, sis," he presently added.

But the younger Miss Day gave no heed to his menace; she addressed herself only, though with all freedom, to Vogelstein. "This is New York; I like it better than Utica."

He had no time to reply, for his servant had arrived with one of the dispensers of fortune; but as he turned away he wondered, in the light of the child's preference, about the towns of the interior. He was naturally exempt from the common doom. The officer who took him in hand, and who had a large straw hat and a diamond breastpin, was quite a man of the world, and in reply to the Count's formal declarations only said, "Well, I guess it's all right; I guess I'll just pass you," distributing chalk-marks as if they had been so many love-pats. The servant had done some superfluous unlocking and unbuckling, and while he closed the pieces the officer stood there wiping his forehead and conversing with Vogelstein. "First visit to our country, sir?—quite alone—no ladies? Of course the ladies are what we're most after." It was in this manner he expressed himself, while the young diplomatist wondered what he was waiting for and whether he ought to slip something into his palm. But this representative of order left our friend only a moment in suspense; he presently turned away with the remark quite paternally uttered, that he hoped the Count would make quite a stay; upon which the young man saw how wrong he should have been to offer a tip. It was simply the American manner, which had a finish of its own after all. Vogelstein's servant had secured a porter with a truck, and he was about to leave the place when he saw Pandora Day dart out of the crowd and address herself with much eagerness to the functionary who had just liberated him. She had an open letter in her hand which she gave him to read and over which he cast his eyes, thoughtfully stroking his beard. Then she led him away to where her parents sat on their luggage. Count Otto sent off his servant with the porter and followed Pandora, to whom he really wished to address a word of farewell. The last thing they had said to each other on the ship was that they should meet again on shore. It seemed improbable however that the meeting would occur anywhere but just here on the dock; inasmuch as Pandora was decidedly not in society, where

Vogelstein would be of course, and as, if Utica—he had her sharp little sister's word for it—was worse than what was about him there, he'd be hanged if he'd go to Utica. He overtook Pandora quickly; she was in the act of introducing the representative of order to her parents, quite in the same manner in which she had introduced the Captain of the ship. Mr. and Mrs. Day got up and shook hands with him and they evidently all prepared to have a little talk. "I should like to introduce you to my brother and sister," he heard the girl say, and he saw her look about for these appendages. He caught her eye as she did so, and advanced with his hand outstretched, reflecting the while that evidently the Americans, whom he had always heard described as silent and practical, rejoiced to extravagance in the social graces. They dawdled and chattered like so many Neapolitans.

"Good-bye, Count Vogelstein," said Pandora, who was a little flushed with her various exertions but didn't look the worse for it. "I hope you'll have a splendid time and appreciate our country."

"I hope you'll get through all right," Vogelstein answered, smiling and feeling himself already more idiomatic.

"That gentleman's sick that I wrote to," she rejoined; "isn't it too bad? But he sent me down a letter to a friend of his—one of the examiners—and I guess we won't have any trouble. Mr. Lansing, let me make you acquainted with Count Vogelstein," she went on, presenting to her fellow-passenger the wearer of the straw hat and the breastpin, who shook hands with the young German as if he had never seen him before. Vogelstein's heart rose for an instant to his throat; he thanked his stars he hadn't offered a tip to the friend of a gentleman who had often been mentioned to him and who had also been described by a member of Pandora's family as Pandora's lover.

"It's a case of ladies this time," Mr. Lansing remarked to him with a smile which seemed to confess surreptitiously, and as if neither party could be eager, to recognition.

"Well, Mr. Bellamy says you'll do anything for *him*," Pandora said, smiling very sweetly at Mr. Lansing. "We haven't got much; we've been gone only two years."

Mr. Lansing scratched his head a little behind, with a movement that sent his straw hat forward in the direction of his nose. "I don't know as I'd do anything for him that I wouldn't do for you," he responded with an equal geniality. "I guess you'd better open that one"—and he gave a little affectionate kick to one of the trunks.

"Oh mother, isn't he lovely? It's only your sea-things," Pandora cried, stooping over the coffer with the key in her hand.

"I don't know as I like showing them," Mrs. Day modestly murmured.

Vogelstein made his German salutation to the company in general, and to Pandora he offered an audible good-bye, which she returned in a bright friendly voice, but without looking round as she fumbled at the lock of her trunk.

"We'll try another, if you like," said Mr. Lansing good-humouredly.

"Oh no it has got to be this one! Good-bye, Count Vogelstein. I hope you'll judge us correctly!"

The young man went his way and passed the barrier of the dock. Here he was met by his English valet with a face of consternation which led him to ask if a cab weren't forthcoming.

"They call 'em 'acks 'ere, sir," said the man, "and they're beyond everything. He wants thirty shillings to take you to the inn."

Vogelstein hesitated a moment. "Couldn't you find a German?"

"By the way he talks he *is* a German!" said the man; and in a moment Count Otto began his career in America by discussing the tariff of hackney-coaches in the language of the fatherland.

## II

HE went wherever he was asked, on principle, partly to study American society and partly because in Washington pastimes seemed to him not so numerous that one could afford to neglect occasions. At the end of two winters he had naturally had a good many of various kinds—his study of American society had yielded considerable fruit. When, however, in April, during the second year of his residence, he presented himself at a large party given by Mrs. Bonnycastle and of which it was believed that it would be the last serious affair of the season, his being there (and still more his looking very fresh and talkative) was not the consequence of a rule of conduct. He went to Mrs. Bonnycastle's simply because he liked the lady, whose receptions were the pleasantest in Washington, and because if he didn't go there he didn't know what he should do; that absence of alternatives having become familiar to him by the waters of the Potomac. There were a great many things he did because if he didn't do them he didn't know what he should do. It must be added that in this case even if there had been an alternative he would still have decided to go to Mrs. Bonnycastle's. If her house wasn't the pleasantest there it was at least difficult to say which was pleasanter; and the complaint sometimes made of it that it was too limited, that it left out, on the whole, more people than it took in, applied with much less force when it was thrown open for a general party. Toward the end of the social year, in those soft scented days of the Washington spring when the air began to show a southern glow and the Squares and Circles (to which the wide empty avenues converged according to a plan so ingenious, yet so bewildering) to flush with pink blossom and to make one wish to sit on benches—under this magic of expansion and condonation Mrs. Bonnycastle, who during the winter had been a good deal on the defensive, relaxed her vigilance a little, became whimsically wilful, vernally reckless, as it were, and ceased to calculate the consequences of an hospitality which a reference to the back files or even to the morning's issue of the newspapers might easily prove a mistake. But Washington life, to Count Otto's apprehension, was paved with mistakes; he felt himself in a society founded on fundamental fallacies and triumphant blunders. Little addicted as he was to the sportive view of existence, he had said to himself at an early stage of his sojourn that the only way to enjoy the great Republic would be to burn one's standards and warm one's self at the blaze. Such were the reflexions of a theoretic Teuton who now walked for the most part amid the ashes of his prejudices.

Mrs. Bonnycastle had endeavoured more than once to explain to him the principles on which she received certain people and ignored certain others; but it was with difficulty that he entered into her discriminations. American promiscuity, goodness knew, had been strange to him, but it was nothing to the queerness of American criticism. This lady would discourse to him *à perte de vue* on differences where he only saw resemblances, and both the merits and the defects of a good many members of Washington society, as this society was interpreted to him by Mrs. Bonnycastle, he was often at a loss to understand. Fortunately she had a fund of good humour which, as I have intimated, was apt to come uppermost with the April blossoms and which made the people she didn't invite to her house almost as amusing to her as those she did. Her husband was not in politics, though politics were much in him; but the couple had taken upon themselves the responsibilities of an active patriotism; they thought it right to live in America, differing therein from many of their acquaintances who only, with some grimness, thought it inevitable. They had that burdensome heritage of foreign reminiscence with which so many Americans were saddled; but they carried it more easily than most of their country-people, and one knew they had lived in Europe only by their present exultation, never in the least by their regrets. Their regrets, that is, were only for their ever having lived there, as Mrs. Bonnycastle once told the wife of a foreign minister. They solved all their problems successfully, including those of knowing none of the people they didn't wish to, and of finding plenty of occupation in a society supposed to be meagrely provided with resources for that body which Vogelstein was to hear invoked, again and again, with the mixture of desire and of deprecation that might have attended the mention of a secret vice, under the name of a leisure-class. When as the warm weather approached they opened both the wings of their house-door, it was because they thought it would entertain them and not because they were conscious of a pressure. Alfred Bonnycastle all winter indeed chafed a little at the definiteness of some of his wife's reserves; it struck him that for Washington their society was really a little too good. Vogelstein still remembered the puzzled feeling—it had cleared up somewhat now—with which, more than a year before, he had heard Mr. Bonnycastle exclaim one evening, after a dinner in his own house, when every guest but the German secretary (who often sat late with the pair) had departed: "Hang it, there's only a month left; let us be vulgar and have some fun—let us invite the President."

This was Mrs. Bonnycastle's carnival, and on the occasion to which I began my chapter by referring the President had not only been invited but had signified his intention of being present. I hasten to add that this was not the same august ruler to whom Alfred Bonnycastle's irreverent allusion had been made. The White House had received a new tenant—the old one was then just leaving it—and Count Otto had had the advantage, during the first eighteen months of his stay in America, of seeing an electoral campaign, a presidential inauguration and a distribution of spoils. He had been bewildered during those first weeks by finding that at the national capital in the houses he supposed to be the best, the head of the State was not a coveted guest; for this could be the only explanation of Mr. Bonnycastle's whimsical suggestion of their inviting him, as it were, in carnival. His successor went out a good deal for a President.

The legislative session was over, but this made little difference in the aspect of Mrs. Bonnycastle's rooms, which even at the height of the congressional season could scarce be said to overflow with the representatives of the people. They were garnished with an occasional Senator, whose movements and utterances often appeared to be regarded with a mixture of alarm and indulgence, as if they would be disappointing if they weren't rather odd and yet might be dangerous if not carefully watched. Our young man had come to entertain a kindness for these conscript fathers of invisible families, who had something of the toga in the voluminous folds of their conversation, but were otherwise rather bare and bald, with stony wrinkles in their faces, like busts and statues of ancient law-givers. There seemed to him something chill and exposed in their being at once so exalted and so naked; there were frequent lonesome glances in their eyes, as if in the social world their legislative consciousness longed for the warmth of a few comfortable laws ready-made. Members of the House were very rare, and when Washington was new to the inquiring secretary he used sometimes to mistake them, in the halls and on the staircases where he met them, for the functionaries engaged, under stress, to usher in guests and wait at supper. It was only a little later that he perceived these latter public characters almost always to be impressive and of that rich racial hue which of itself served as a livery. At present, however, such confounding figures were much less to be met than during the months of winter, and indeed they were never frequent at Mrs. Bonnycastle's. At present the social vistas of Washington, like the vast fresh flatness of the lettered and numbered streets, which at this season seemed to Vogelstein more spacious and vague than ever, suggested but a paucity of political phenomena. Count Otto that evening knew every one or almost every one. There were often inquiring strangers, expecting great things, from New York and Boston, and to them, in the friendly Washington way, the young German was promptly introduced. It was a society in which familiarity reigned and in which people were liable to meet three times a day, so that their ultimate essence really became a matter of importance.

"I've got three new girls," Mrs. Bonnycastle said. "You must talk to them all."

"All at once?" Vogelstein asked, reversing in fancy a position not at all unknown to him. He had so repeatedly heard himself addressed in even more than triple simultaneity.

"Oh no; you must have something different for each; you can't get off that way. Haven't you discovered that the American girl expects something especially adapted to herself? It's very well for Europe to have a few phrases that will do for any girl. The American girl isn't *any* girl; she's a remarkable specimen in a remarkable species. But you must keep the best this evening for Miss Day."

"For Miss Day!"—and Vogelstein had a stare of intelligence. "Do you mean for Pandora?"

Mrs. Bonnycastle broke on her side into free amusement. "One would think you had been looking for her over the globe! So you know her already— and you call her by her pet name?"

"Oh no, I don't know her; that is I haven't seen her or thought of her from that day to this. We came to America in the same ship."

"Isn't she an American then?"

"Oh yes; she lives at Utica—in the interior."

"In the interior of Utica? You can't mean my young woman then, who lives in New York, where she's a great beauty and a great belle and has been immensely admired this winter."

"After all," said Count Otto, considering and a little disappointed, "the name's not so uncommon; it's perhaps another. But has she rather strange eyes, a little yellow, but very pretty, and a nose a little arched?"

"I can't tell you all that; I haven't seen her. She's staying with Mrs. Steuben. She only came a day or two ago, and Mrs. Steuben's to bring her. When she wrote to me to ask leave she told me what I tell you. They haven't come yet."

Vogelstein felt a quick hope that the subject of this correspondence might indeed be the young lady he had parted from on the dock at New York, but the indications seemed to point another way, and he had no wish to cherish an illusion. It didn't seem to him probable that the energetic girl who had introduced him to Mr. Lansing would have the entrée of the best house in Washington; besides, Mrs. Bonnycastle's guest was described as a beauty and belonging to the brilliant city.

"What's the social position of Mrs. Steuben?" it occurred to him to ask while he meditated. He had an earnest artless literal way of putting such a question as that; you could see from it that he was very thorough.

34

Mrs. Bonnycastle met it, however, but, with mocking laughter. "I'm sure I don't know! What's your own?"—and she left him to turn to her other guests, to several of whom she repeated his question. Could they tell her what was the social position of Mrs. Steuben? There was Count Vogelstein who wanted to know. He instantly became aware of course that he oughtn't so to have expressed himself. Wasn't the lady's place in the scale sufficiently indicated by Mrs. Bonnycastle's acquaintance with her? Still there were fine degrees, and he felt a little unduly snubbed. It was perfectly true, as he told his hostess, that with the quick wave of new impressions that had rolled over him after his arrival in America the image of Pandora was almost completely effaced; he had seen innumerable things that were quite as remarkable in their way as the heroine of the *Donau*, but at the touch of the idea that he might see her and hear her again at any moment she became as vivid in his mind as if they had parted the day before: he remembered the exact shade of the eyes he had described to Mrs. Bonnycastle as yellow, the tone of her voice when at the last she expressed the hope he might judge America correctly. *Had* he judged America correctly? If he were to meet her again she doubtless would try to ascertain. It would be going much too far to say that the idea of such an ordeal was terrible to Count Otto; but it may at least be said that the thought of meeting Pandora Day made him nervous. The fact is certainly singular, but I shall not take on myself to explain it; there are some things that even the most philosophic historian isn't bound to account for.

He wandered into another room, and there, at the end of five minutes, he was introduced by Mrs. Bonnycastle to one of the young ladies of whom she had spoken. This was a very intelligent girl who came from Boston and showed much acquaintance with Spielhagen's novels. "Do you like them?" Vogelstein asked rather vaguely, not taking much interest in the matter, as he read works of fiction only in case of a sea-voyage. The young lady from Boston looked pensive and concentrated; then she answered that she liked *some* of them *very* much, but that there were others she didn't like—and she enumerated the works that came under each of these heads. Spielhagen is a voluminous writer, and such a catalogue took some time; at the end of it moreover Vogelstein's question was not answered, for he couldn't have told us whether she liked Spielhagen or not.

On the next topic, however, there was no doubt about her feelings. They talked about Washington as people talk only in the place itself, revolving about the subject in widening and narrowing circles, perching successively on its many branches, considering it from every point of view. Our young man had been long enough in America to discover that after half a century of social neglect Washington had become the fashion and enjoyed the great advantage of being a new resource in conversation. This was especially the case in the months of spring, when the inhabitants of the commercial cities came so far southward to escape, after the long winter, that final affront. They were all agreed that Washington was fascinating, and none of them were better prepared to talk it over than the Bostonians. Vogelstein originally had been rather out of step with them; he hadn't seized their point of view, hadn't known with what they compared this object of their infatuation. But now he knew everything; he had settled down to the pace; there wasn't a possible phase of the discussion that could find him at a loss. There was a kind of Hegelian element in it; in the light of these considerations the American capital took on the semblance of a monstrous mystical infinite *Werden*. But they fatigued Vogelstein a little, and it was his preference, as a general thing, not to engage the same evening with more than one newcomer, one visitor in the freshness of initiation. This was why Mrs. Bonnycastle's expression of a wish to introduce him to three young ladies had startled him a little; he saw a certain process, in which he flattered himself that he had become proficient, but which was after all tolerably exhausting, repeated for each of the damsels. After separating from his judicious Bostonian he rather evaded Mrs. Bonnycastle, contenting himself with the conversation of old friends, pitched for the most part in a lower and easier key.

At last he heard it mentioned that the President had arrived, had been some half-hour in the house, and he went in search of the illustrious guest, whose whereabouts at Washington parties was never indicated by a cluster of courtiers. He made it a point, whenever he found himself in company with the President, to pay him his respects, and he had not been discouraged by the fact that there was no association of ideas in the eye of the great man as he put out his hand presidentially and said, "Happy to meet you, sir." Count Otto felt himself taken for a mere loyal subject, possibly for an office-seeker; and he used to reflect at such moments that the monarchical form had its merits it provided a line of heredity for the faculty of quick recognition. He had now some difficulty in finding the chief magistrate, and ended by learning that he was in the tea-room, a small apartment devoted to light refection near the entrance of the house. Here our young man presently perceived him seated on a sofa and in conversation with a lady. There were a number of people about the table, eating, drinking, talking; and the couple on the sofa, which was not near it but against the wall, in a shallow recess, looked a little withdrawn, as if they had sought seclusion and were disposed to profit by the diverted attention of the others. The President leaned back; his gloved hands, resting on either knee, made large white spots. He looked eminent, but he looked relaxed, and the lady beside him ministered freely and without scruple, it was clear, to this effect of his comfortably unbending. Vogelstein caught her voice as he approached. He heard her say "Well now, remember; I consider it a promise." She was beautifully dressed, in rose-colour; her hands were clasped in her lap and her eyes attached to the presidential profile.

"Well, madam, in that case it's about the fiftieth promise I've given to-day."

It was just as he heard these words, uttered by her companion in reply, that Count Otto checked himself, turned away and pretended to be looking for a cup of tea. It wasn't usual to disturb the President, even simply to shake hands, when he was sitting on a sofa with a lady, and the young secretary felt it in this case less possible than ever to break the rule, for the lady on the sofa was none other than Pandora Day. He had recognised her without her appearing to see him, and even with half an eye, as they said, had taken in that she was now a person to be reckoned with. She had an air of elation, of success; she shone, to intensity, in her rose-coloured dress; she was extracting promises from the ruler of fifty millions of people. What an odd place to meet her, her old shipmate thought, and how little one could tell, after all, in America, who people were! He didn't want to speak to her yet; he wanted to wait a little and learn more; but meanwhile there was something attractive in the fact that she was just behind him, a few yards off, that if he should turn he might see her again. It was she Mrs. Bonnycastle had meant, it was she who was so much admired in New York. Her face was the same, yet he had made out in a moment that she was vaguely prettier; he had recognised the arch of her nose, which suggested a fine ambition. He took some tea, which he hadn't desired, in order not to go away. He remembered her *entourage* on the steamer; her father and mother, the silent senseless burghers, so little "of the world," her infant sister, so much of it, her humorous brother with his tall hat and his influence in the smoking-room. He remembered Mrs. Dangerfield's warnings—yet her perplexities too—and the letter from Mr. Bellamy, and the introduction to Mr. Lansing, and the way Pandora had stooped down on the dirty dock, laughing and talking, mistress of the situation, to open her trunk for the Customs. He was pretty sure she had paid no duties that day; this would naturally have been the purpose of Mr. Bellamy's letter. Was she still in correspondence with that gentleman, and had he got over the sickness interfering with their reunion? These images and these questions coursed through Count Otto's mind, and he saw it must be quite in Pandora's line to be mistress of the situation, for there was evidently nothing on the present occasion that could call itself her master. He drank his tea and as; he put down his cup heard the President, behind him, say: "Well, I guess my wife will wonder why I don't come home."

"Why didn't you bring her with you?" Pandora benevolently asked.

"Well, she doesn't go out much. Then she has got her sister staying with her—Mrs. Runkle, from Natchez. She's a good deal of an invalid, and my wife doesn't like to leave her."

"She must be a very kind woman"—and there was a high mature competence in the way the girl sounded the note of approval.

"Well, I guess she isn't spoiled—yet."

"I should like very much to come and see her," said Pandora.

"Do come round. Couldn't you come some night?" the great man responded.

"Well, I'll come some time. And I shall remind you of your promise."

"All right. There's nothing like keeping it up. Well," said the President, "I must bid good-bye to these bright folks."

Vogelstein heard him rise from the sofa with his companion; after which he gave the pair time to pass out of the room before him. They did it with a certain impressive deliberation, people making way for the ruler of fifty millions and looking with a certain curiosity at the striking pink person at his side. When a little later he followed them across the hall, into one of the other rooms, he saw the host and hostess accompany the President to the door and two foreign ministers and a judge of the Supreme Court address themselves to Pandora Day. He resisted the impulse to join this circle: if he should speak to her at all he would somehow wish it to be in more privacy. She continued nevertheless to occupy him, and when Mrs. Bonnycastle came back from the hall he immediately approached her with an appeal. "I wish you'd tell me something more about that girl—that one opposite and in pink."

"The lovely Day—that's what they call her, I believe? I wanted you to talk with her."

"I find she is the one I've met. But she seems to be so different here. I can't make it out," said Count Otto.

There was something in his expression that again moved Mrs. Bonnycastle to mirth. "How we do puzzle you Europeans! You look quite bewildered."

"I'm sorry I look so—I try to hide it. But of course we're very simple. Let me ask then a simple earnest childlike question. Are her parents also in society?"

"Parents in society? D'où tombez-vous? Did you ever hear of the parents of a triumphant girl in rose-colour, with a nose all her own, in society?"

"Is she then all alone?" he went on with a strain of melancholy in his voice.

Mrs. Bonnycastle launched at him all her laughter.

"You're too pathetic. Don't you know what she is? I supposed of course you knew."

"It's exactly what I'm asking you."

"Why she's the new type. It has only come up lately. They have had articles about it in the papers. That's the reason I told Mrs. Steuben to bring her."

"The new type? *What* new type, Mrs. Bonnycastle?" he returned pleadingly—so conscious was he that all types in America were new.

Her laughter checked her reply a moment, and by the time she had recovered herself the young lady from Boston, with whom Vogelstein had been talking, stood there to take leave. This, for an American type, was an old one, he was sure; and the process of parting between the guest and her hostess had an ancient elaboration. Count Otto waited a little; then he turned away and walked up to Pandora Day, whose group of interlocutors had now been re-enforced by a gentleman who had held an important place in the cabinet of the late occupant of the presidential chair. He had asked Mrs. Bonnycastle if she were "all alone"; but there was nothing in her present situation to show her for solitary. She wasn't sufficiently alone for our friend's taste; but he was impatient and he hoped she'd give him a few words to himself. She recognised him without a moment's hesitation and with the sweetest smile, a smile matching to a shade the tone in which she said: "I was watching you. I wondered if you weren't going to speak to me."

"Miss Day was watching him!" one of the foreign ministers exclaimed; "and we flattered ourselves that her attention was all with us."

"I mean before," said the girl, "while I was talking with the President."

At which the gentlemen began to laugh, one of them remarking that this was the way the absent were sacrificed, even the great; while another put on record that he hoped Vogelstein was duly flattered.

"Oh I was watching the President too," said Pandora. "I've got to watch *him*. He has promised me something."

"It must be the mission to England," the judge of the Supreme Court suggested. "A good position for a lady; they've got a lady at the head over there."

"I wish they would send you to my country," one of the foreign ministers suggested. "I'd immediately get recalled."

"Why perhaps in your country I wouldn't speak to you! It's only because you're here," the ex-heroine of the *Donau* returned with a gay familiarity which evidently ranked with her but as one of the arts of defence. "You'll see what mission it is when it comes out. But I'll speak to Count Vogelstein anywhere," she went on. "He's an older friend than any right here. I've known him in difficult days."

"Oh yes, on the great ocean," the young man smiled. "On the watery waste, in the tempest!"

"Oh I don't mean that so much; we had a beautiful voyage and there wasn't any tempest. I mean when I was living in Utica. That's a watery waste if you like, and a tempest there would have been a pleasant variety."

"Your parents seemed to me so peaceful!" her associate in the other memories sighed with a vague wish to say something sympathetic.

"Oh you haven't seen them ashore! At Utica they were very lively. But that's no longer our natural home. Don't you remember I told you I was working for New York? Well, I worked—I had to work hard. But we've moved."

Count Otto clung to his interest. "And I hope they're happy."

"My father and mother? Oh they will be, in time. I must give them time. They're very young yet, they've years before them. And you've been always in Washington?" Pandora continued. "I suppose you've found out everything about everything."

"Oh no—there are some things I *can't* find out."

41

"Come and see me and perhaps I can help you. I'm very different from what I was in that phase. I've advanced a great deal since then."

"Oh how was Miss Day in that phase?" asked a cabinet minister of the last administration.

"She was delightful of course," Count Otto said.

"He's very flattering; I didn't open my mouth!" Pandora cried. "Here comes Mrs. Steuben to take me to some other place. I believe it's a literary party near the Capitol. Everything seems so separate in Washington. Mrs. Steuben's going to read a poem. I wish she'd read it here; wouldn't it do as well?"

This lady, arriving, signified to her young friend the necessity of their moving on. But Miss Day's companions had various things to say to her before giving her up. She had a vivid answer for each, and it was brought home to Vogelstein while he listened that this would be indeed, in her development, as she said, another phase. Daughter of small burghers as she might be she was really brilliant. He turned away a little and while Mrs. Steuben waited put her a question. He had made her half an hour before the subject of that inquiry to which Mrs. Bonnycastle returned so ambiguous an answer; but this wasn't because he failed of all direct acquaintance with the amiable woman or of any general idea of the esteem in which she was held. He had met her in various places and had been at her house. She was the widow of a commodore, was a handsome mild soft swaying person, whom every one liked, with glossy bands of black hair and a little ringlet depending behind each ear. Some one had said that she looked like the *vieux jeu*, idea of the queen in *Hamlet*. She had written verses which were admired in the South, wore a full-length portrait of the commodore on her bosom and spoke with the accent of Savannah. She had about her a positive strong odour of Washington. It had certainly been very superfluous in our young man to question Mrs. Bonnycastle about her social position.

"Do kindly tell me," he said, lowering his voice, "what's the type to which that young lady belongs? Mrs. Bonnycastle tells me it's a new one."

Mrs. Steuben for a moment fixed her liquid eyes on the secretary of legation. She always seemed to be translating the prose of your speech into the finer rhythms with which her own mind was familiar. "Do you think anything's really new?" she then began to flute. "I'm very fond of the old; you know that's a weakness of we Southerners." The poor lady, it will be observed, had another weakness as well. "What we often take to be the new is simply the old under some novel form. Were there not remarkable natures in the past? If you doubt it you should visit the South, where the past still lingers."

Vogelstein had been struck before this with Mrs. Steuben's pronunciation of the word by which her native latitudes were designated; transcribing it from her lips you would have written it (as the nearest approach) the Sooth. But at present he scarce heeded this peculiarity; he was wondering rather how a woman could be at once so copious and so uninforming. What did he care about the past or even about the Sooth? He was afraid of starting her again. He looked at her, discouraged and helpless, as bewildered almost as Mrs. Bonnycastle had found him half an hour before; looked also at the commodore, who, on her bosom, seemed to breathe again with his widow's respirations. "Call it an old type then if you like," he said in a moment. "All I want to know is what type it *is*! It seems impossible," he gasped, "to find out."

"You can find out in the newspapers. They've had articles about it. They write about everything now. But it isn't true about Miss Day. It's one of the first families. Her great-grandfather was in the Revolution." Pandora by this time had given her attention again to Mrs. Steuben. She seemed to signify that she was ready to move on. "Wasn't your great-grandfather in the Revolution?" the elder lady asked. "I'm telling Count Vogelstein about him."

"Why are you asking about my ancestors?" the girl demanded of the young German with untempered brightness. "Is that the thing you said just now that you can't find out? Well, if Mrs. Steuben will only be quiet you never will."

Mrs. Steuben shook her head rather dreamily. "Well, it's no trouble for we of the Sooth to be quiet. There's a kind of languor in our blood. Besides, we have to be to-day. But I've got to show some energy to-night. I've got to get you to the end of Pennsylvania Avenue."

Pandora gave her hand to Count Otto and asked him if he thought they should meet again. He answered that in Washington people were always meeting again and that at any rate he shouldn't fail to wait upon her. Hereupon, just as the two ladies were detaching themselves, Mrs. Steuben remarked that if the Count and Miss Day wished to meet again the picnic would be a good chance—the picnic she was getting up for the following Thursday. It was to consist of about twenty bright people, and they'd go down the Potomac to Mount Vernon. The Count answered that if Mrs. Steuben thought him bright enough he should be delighted to join the party; and he was told the hour for which the tryst was taken.

He remained at Mrs. Bonnycastle's after every one had gone, and then he informed this lady of his reason for waiting. Would she have mercy on him and let him know, in a single word, before he went to rest—for without it rest would be impossible—what was this famous type to which Pandora Day belonged?

"Gracious, you don't mean to say you've not found out that type yet!" Mrs. Bonnycastle exclaimed with a return of her hilarity. "What have you been doing all the evening? You Germans may be thorough, but you certainly are not quick!"

It was Alfred Bonnycastle who at last took pity on him. "My dear Vogelstein, she's the latest freshest fruit of our great American evolution. She's the self-made girl!"

Count Otto gazed a moment. "The fruit of the great American Revolution? Yes, Mrs. Steuben told me her great-grandfather—" but the rest of his sentence was lost in a renewed explosion of Mrs. Bonnycastle's sense of the ridiculous. He bravely pushed his advantage, such as it was, however, and, desiring his host's definition to be defined, inquired what the self-made girl might be.

"Sit down and we'll tell you all about it," Mrs. Bonnycastle said. "I like talking this way, after a party's over. You can smoke if you like, and Alfred will open another window. Well, to begin with, the self-made girl's a new feature.

That, however, you know. In the second place she isn't self-made at all. We all help to make her—we take such an interest in her."

"That's only after she's made!" Alfred Bonnycastle broke in. "But it's Vogelstein that takes an interest. What on earth has started you up so on the subject of Miss Day?"

The visitor explained as well as he could that it was merely the accident of his having crossed the ocean in the steamer with her; but he felt the inadequacy of this account of the matter, felt it more than his hosts, who could know neither how little actual contact he had had with her on the ship, how much he had been affected by Mrs. Dangerfield's warnings, nor how much observation at the same time he had lavished on her. He sat there half an hour, and the warm dead stillness of the Washington night—nowhere are the nights so silent—came in at the open window, mingled with a soft sweet earthy smell, the smell of growing things and in particular, as he thought, of Mrs. Steuben's Sooth. Before he went away he had heard all about the self-made girl, and there was something in the picture that strongly impressed him. She was possible doubtless only in America; American life had smoothed the way for her. She was not fast, nor emancipated, nor crude, nor loud, and there wasn't in her, of necessity at least, a grain of the stuff of which the adventuress is made. She was simply very successful, and her success was entirely personal. She hadn't been born with the silver spoon of social opportunity; she had grasped it by honest exertion. You knew her by many different signs, but chiefly, infallibly, by the appearance of her parents. It was her parents who told her story; you always saw how little her parents could have made her. Her attitude with regard to them might vary in different ways. As the great fact on her own side was that she had lifted herself from a lower social plane, done it all herself, and done it by the simple lever of her personality, it was naturally to be expected that she would leave the authors of her mere material being in the shade. Sometimes she had them in her wake, lost in the bubbles and the foam that showed where she had passed; sometimes, as Alfred Bonnycastle said, she let them slide altogether; sometimes she kept them in close confinement, resorting to them under cover of night and with every precaution; sometimes she exhibited them to the public in discreet glimpses, in prearranged attitudes. But the general characteristic of the self-made girl was that, though it was frequently understood that she was privately devoted to her kindred, she never attempted to impose them on society, and it was striking that, though in some of her manifestations a bore, she was at her worst less of a bore than they. They were almost always solemn and portentous, and they were for the most part of a deathly respectability. She wasn't necessarily snobbish, unless it was snobbish to want the best. She didn't cringe, she didn't make herself smaller than she was; she took on the contrary a stand of her own and attracted things to herself. Naturally she was possible only in America—only in a country where whole ranges of competition and comparison were absent. The natural history of this interesting creature was at last completely laid bare to the earnest stranger, who, as he sat there in the animated stillness, with the fragrant breath of the Western world in his nostrils, was convinced of what he had already suspected, that conversation in the great Republic was more yearningly, not to say gropingly, psychological than elsewhere. Another thing, as he learned, that you knew the self-made girl by was her culture, which was perhaps a little too restless and obvious. She had usually got into society more or less by reading, and her conversation was apt to be garnished with literary allusions, even with familiar quotations. Vogelstein hadn't had time to observe this element as a developed form in Pandora Day; but Alfred Bonnycastle hinted that he wouldn't trust her to keep it under in a *tête-à-tête*. It was needless to say that these young persons had always been to Europe; that was usually the first place they got to. By such arts they sometimes entered society on the other side before they did so at home; it was to be added at the same time that this resource was less and less valuable, for Europe, in the American world, had less and less prestige and people in the Western hemisphere now kept a watch on that roundabout road. All of which quite applied to Pandora Day—the journey to Europe, the culture (as exemplified in the books she read on the ship), the relegation, the effacement, of the family. The only thing that was exceptional was the rapidity of her march; for the jump she had taken since he left her in the hands of Mr. Lansing struck Vogelstein, even after he had made all allowance for the abnormal homogeneity of the American mass, as really considerable. It took all her cleverness to account for such things. When she "moved" from

Utica—mobilised her commissariat—the battle appeared virtually to have been gained.

Count Otto called the next day, and Mrs. Steuben's blackamoor informed him, in the communicative manner of his race, that the ladies had gone out to pay some visits and look at the Capitol. Pandora apparently had not hitherto examined this monument, and our young man wished he had known, the evening before, of her omission, so that he might have offered to be her initiator. There is too obvious a connexion for us to fail of catching it between his regret and the fact that in leaving Mrs. Steuben's door he reminded himself that he wanted a good walk, and that he thereupon took his way along Pennsylvania Avenue. His walk had become fairly good by the time he reached the great white edifice that unfolds its repeated colonnades and uplifts its isolated dome at the end of a long vista of saloons and tobacco-shops. He slowly climbed the great steps, hesitating a little, even wondering why he had come. The superficial reason was obvious enough, but there was a real one behind it that struck him as rather wanting in the solidity which should characterise the motives of an emissary of Prince Bismarck. The superficial reason was a belief that Mrs. Steuben would pay her visit first—it was probably only a question of leaving cards—and bring her young friend to the Capitol at the hour when the yellow afternoon light would give a tone to the blankness of its marble walls. The Capitol was a splendid building, but it was rather wanting in tone. Vogelstein's curiosity about Pandora Day had been much more quickened than checked by the revelations made to him in Mrs. Bonnycastle's drawing-room. It was a relief to have the creature classified; but he had a desire, of which he had not been conscious before, to see really to the end how well, in other words how completely and artistically, a girl could make herself. His calculations had been just, and he had wandered about the rotunda for only ten minutes, looking again at the paintings, commemorative of the national annals, which occupy its lower spaces, and at the simulated sculptures, so touchingly characteristic of early American taste, which adorn its upper reaches, when the charming women he had been counting on presented themselves in charge of a licensed guide. He went to meet them and didn't conceal from them that he had marked them for his very own. The encounter was happy on both sides, and he accompanied them through the queer and endless interior, through labyrinths of bleak bare development, into legislative and judicial halls. He thought it a hideous place; he had seen it all before and asked himself what senseless game he was playing. In the lower House were certain bedaubed walls, in the basest style of imitation, which made him feel faintly sick, not to speak of a lobby adorned with artless prints and photographs of eminent defunct Congressmen that was all too serious for a joke and too comic for a Valhalla. But Pandora was greatly interested; she thought the Capitol very fine; it was easy to criticise the details, but as a whole it was the most impressive building she had ever seen. She proved a charming fellow tourist; she had constantly something to say, but never said it too much; it was impossible to drag in the wake of a *cicerone* less of a lengthening or an irritating chain. Vogelstein could see too that she wished to improve her mind; she looked at the historical pictures, at the uncanny statues of local worthies, presented by the different States—they were of different sizes, as if they had been "numbered," in a shop—she asked questions of the guide and in the chamber of the Senate requested him to show her the chairs of the gentlemen from New York. She sat down in one of them, though Mrs. Steuben told her *that* Senator (she mistook the chair, dropping into another State) was a horrid old thing.

Throughout the hour he spent with her Vogelstein seemed to see how it was she had made herself. They walked about, afterwards on the splendid terrace that surrounds the Capitol, the great marble floor on which it stands, and made vague remarks—Pandora's were the most definite—about the yellow sheen of the Potomac, the hazy hills of Virginia, the far-gleaming pediment of Arlington, the raw confused-looking country. Washington was beneath them, bristling and geometrical; the long lines of its avenues seemed to stretch into national futures. Pandora asked Count Otto if he had ever been to Athens and, on his admitting so much, sought to know whether the eminence on which they stood didn't give him an idea of the Acropolis in its prime. Vogelstein deferred the satisfaction of this appeal to their next meeting; he was glad—in spite of the appeal—to make pretexts for seeing her again. He did so on the morrow; Mrs. Steuben's picnic was still three days distant. He called on Pandora a second time, also met her each evening in the Washington world. It took very little of this to remind him that he was forgetting both Mrs. Dangerfield's warnings and the admonitions—long familiar to him—of his own conscience. Was he in peril of love? Was he to be sacrificed on the altar of the American girl, an altar at which those other poor fellows had poured out some of the bluest blood in Germany and he had himself taken oath he would never seriously worship? He decided that he wasn't in real danger, that he had rather clinched his precautions. It was true that a young person who had succeeded so well for herself might be a great help to her husband; but this diplomatic aspirant preferred on the whole that his success should be his own: it wouldn't please him to have the air of being pushed by his wife. Such a wife as that would wish to push him, and he could hardly admit to himself that this was what fate had in reserve for him—to be propelled in his career by a young lady who would perhaps attempt to talk to the Kaiser as he had heard her the other night talk to the President. Would she consent to discontinue relations with her family, or would she wish still to borrow plastic relief from that domestic background? That her family was so impossible was to a certain extent an advantage; for if they had been a little better the question of a rupture would be less easy. He turned over these questions in spite of his security, or perhaps indeed because of it. The security made them speculative and disinterested.

They haunted him during the excursion to Mount Vernon, which took place according to traditions long established. Mrs. Steuben's confederates assembled on the steamer and were set afloat on the big brown stream which had already seemed to our special traveller to have too much bosom and too little bank. Here and there, however, he became conscious of a shore where there was something to look at, even though conscious at the same time that he had of old lost great opportunities of an idyllic cast in not having managed to be more "thrown with" a certain young lady on the deck of the North German Lloyd. The two turned round together to hang over Alexandria, which for Pandora, as she declared, was a picture of Old Virginia. She told Vogelstein that she was always hearing about it during the Civil War, ages before. Little girl as she had been at the time she remembered all the names

49

that were on people's lips during those years of reiteration. This historic spot had a touch of the romance of rich decay, a reference to older things, to a dramatic past. The past of Alexandria appeared in the vista of three or four short streets sloping up a hill and lined with poor brick warehouses erected for merchandise that had ceased to come or go. It looked hot and blank and sleepy, down to the shabby waterside where tattered darkies dangled their bare feet from the edge of rotting wharves. Pandora was even more interested in Mount Vernon—when at last its wooded bluff began to command the river—than she had been in the Capitol, and after they had disembarked and ascended to the celebrated mansion she insisted on going into every room it contained. She "claimed for it," as she said—some of her turns were so characteristic both of her nationality and her own style—the finest situation in the world, and was distinct as to the shame of their not giving it to the President for his country-seat. Most of her companions had seen the house often, and were now coupling themselves in the grounds according to their sympathies, so that it was easy for Vogelstein to offer the benefit of his own experience to the most inquisitive member of the party. They were not to lunch for another hour, and in the interval the young man roamed with his first and fairest acquaintance. The breath of the Potomac, on the boat, had been a little harsh, but on the softly-curving lawn, beneath the clustered trees, with the river relegated to a mere shining presence far below and in the distance, the day gave out nothing but its mildness, the whole scene became noble and genial.

Count Otto could joke a little on great occasions, and the present one was worthy of his humour. He maintained to his companion that the shallow painted mansion resembled a false house, a "wing" or structure of daubed canvas, on the stage; but she answered him so well with certain economical palaces she had seen in Germany, where, as she said, there was nothing but china stoves and stuffed birds, that he was obliged to allow the home of Washington to be after all really *gemüthlich*. What he found so in fact was the soft texture of the day, his personal situation, the sweetness of his suspense. For suspense had decidedly become his portion; he was under a charm that made him feel he was watching his own life and that his susceptibilities were beyond his control. It hung over him that things might take a turn, from one hour to the other, which would make them very different from what they had been yet; and his heart certainly beat a little faster as he wondered what that turn might be. Why did he come to picnics on fragrant April days with American girls who might lead him too far? Wouldn't such girls be glad to marry a Pomeranian count? And *would* they, after all, talk that way to the Kaiser? If he were to marry one of them he should have to give her several thorough lessons.

In their little tour of the house our young friend and his companion had had a great many fellow visitors, who had also arrived by the steamer and who had hitherto not left them an ideal privacy. But the others gradually dispersed; they circled about a kind of showman who was the authorised guide, a big slow genial vulgar heavily-bearded man, with a whimsical edifying patronising tone, a tone that had immense success when he stopped here and there to make his points—to pass his eyes over his listening flock, then fix them quite above it with a meditative look and bring out some ancient pleasantry as if it were a sudden inspiration. He made a cheerful thing, an echo of the platform before the booth of a country fair, even of a visit to the tomb of the *pater patriæ*. It is enshrined in a kind of grotto in the grounds, and Vogelstein remarked to Pandora that he was a good man for the place, but was too familiar. "Oh he'd have been familiar with Washington," said the girl with the bright dryness with which she often uttered amusing things. Vogelstein looked at her a moment, and it came over him, as he smiled, that she herself probably wouldn't have been abashed even by the hero with whom history has taken fewest liberties. "You look as if you could hardly believe that," Pandora went on. "You Germans are always in such awe of great people." And it occurred to her critic that perhaps after all Washington would have liked her manner, which was wonderfully fresh and natural. The man with the beard was an ideal minister to American shrines; he played on the curiosity of his little band with the touch of a master, drawing them at the right moment away to see the classic ice-house where the old lady had been found weeping in the belief it was Washington's grave. While this monument was under inspection our interesting couple had the house to themselves, and they spent some time on a pretty terrace where certain windows of the second floor opened—a little rootless verandah which overhung, in a manner, obliquely, all the magnificence of the view; the immense sweep of the river, the artistic plantations, the last-century garden with its big box hedges and remains of old espaliers. They lingered here for nearly half an hour, and it was in this retirement that Vogelstein enjoyed the only approach to intimate conversation appointed for him, as was to appear, with a young woman in whom he had been unable to persuade himself that he was not absorbed. It's not necessary, and it's not possible, that I should reproduce this colloquy; but I may mention that it began—as they leaned against the parapet of the terrace and heard the cheerful voice of the showman wafted up to them from a distance—with his saying to her rather abruptly that he couldn't make out why they hadn't had more talk together when they crossed the Atlantic.

"Well, I can if you can't," said Pandora. "I'd have talked quick enough if you had spoken to me. I spoke to you first."

"Yes, I remember that"—and it affected him awkwardly.

"You listened too much to Mrs. Dangerfield."

He feigned a vagueness. "To Mrs. Dangerfield?"

"That woman you were always sitting with; she told you not to speak to me. I've seen her in New York; she speaks to me now herself. She recommended you to have nothing to do with me."

"Oh how can you say such dreadful things?" Count Otto cried with a very becoming blush.

"You know you can't deny it. You weren't attracted by my family. They're charming people when you know them. I don't have a better time anywhere than I have at home," the girl went on loyally. "But what does it matter? My family are very happy. They're getting quite used to New York. Mrs. Dangerfield's a vulgar wretch—next winter she'll call on me."

"You are unlike any Mädchen I've ever seen—I don't understand you," said poor Vogelstein with the colour still in his face.

"Well, you never *will* understand me—probably; but what difference does it make?"

He attempted to tell her what difference, but I've no space to follow him here. It's known that when the German mind attempts to explain things it doesn't always reduce them to simplicity, and Pandora was first mystified, then amused, by some of the Count's revelations. At last I think she was a little frightened, for she remarked irrelevantly, with some decision, that luncheon would be ready and that they ought to join Mrs. Steuben. Her companion walked slowly, on purpose, as they left the house together, for he knew the pang of a vague sense that he was losing her.

"And shall you be in Washington many days yet?" he appealed as they went.

"It will all depend. I'm expecting important news. What I shall do will be influenced by that."

The way she talked about expecting news—and important!—made him feel somehow that she had a career, that she was active and independent, so that he could scarcely hope to stop her as she passed. It was certainly true that he had never seen any girl like her. It would have occurred to him that the news she was expecting might have reference to the favour she had begged of the President, if he hadn't already made up his mind—in the calm of meditation after that talk with the Bonnycastles—that this favour must be a pleasantry. What she had said to him had a discouraging, a somewhat chilling effect; nevertheless it was not without a certain ardour that he inquired of her whether, so long as she stayed in Washington, he mightn't pay her certain respectful attentions.

"As many as you like—and as respectful ones; but you won't keep them up for ever!"

"You try to torment me," said Count Otto.

She waited to explain. "I mean that I may have some of my family."

"I shall be delighted to see them again."

Again she just hung fire. "There are some you've never seen."

In the afternoon, returning to Washington on the steamer, Vogelstein received a warning. It came from Mrs. Bonnycastle and constituted, oddly enough, the second juncture at which an officious female friend had, while sociably afloat with him, advised him on the subject of Pandora Day.

"There's one thing we forgot to tell you the other night about the self-made girl," said the lady of infinite mirth. "It's never safe to fix your affections on her, because she has almost always an impediment somewhere in the background."

He looked at her askance, but smiled and said: "I should understand your information—for which I'm so much obliged—a little better if I knew what you mean by an impediment."

"Oh I mean she's always engaged to some young man who belongs to her earlier phase."

"Her earlier phase?"

"The time before she had made herself—when she lived unconscious of her powers. A young man from Utica, say. They usually have to wait; he's probably in a store. It's a long engagement."

Count Otto somehow preferred to understand as little as possible. "Do you mean a betrothal—to take effect?"

"I don't mean anything German and moonstruck. I mean that piece of peculiarly American enterprise a premature engagement—to take effect, but too complacently, at the end of time."

Vogelstein very properly reflected that it was no use his having entered the diplomatic career if he weren't able to bear himself as if this interesting generalisation had no particular message for him. He did Mrs. Bonnycastle moreover the justice to believe that she wouldn't have approached the question with such levity if she had supposed she should make him wince. The whole thing was, like everything else, but for her to laugh at, and the betrayal moreover of a good intention. "I see, I see—the self-made girl has of course always had a past. Yes, and the young man in the store—from Utica—is part of her past."

"You express it perfectly," said Mrs. Bonnycastle. "I couldn't say it better myself."

"But with her present, with her future, when they change like this young lady's, I suppose everything else changes. How do you say it in America? She lets him slide."

"We don't say it at all!" Mrs. Bonnycastle cried. "She does nothing of the sort; for what do you take her? She sticks to him; that at least is what we *expect* her to do," she added with less assurance. "As I tell you, the type's new and the case under consideration. We haven't yet had time for complete study."

"Oh of course I hope she sticks to him," Vogelstein declared simply and with his German accent more audible, as it always was when he was slightly agitated.

For the rest of the trip he was rather restless. He wandered about the boat, talking little with the returning picnickers. Toward the last, as they drew near Washington and the white dome of the Capitol hung aloft before them, looking as simple as a suspended snowball, he found himself, on the deck, in proximity to Mrs. Steuben. He reproached himself with having rather neglected her during an entertainment for which he was indebted to her bounty, and he sought to repair his omission by a proper deference. But the only act of homage that occurred to him was to ask her as by chance whether Miss Day were, to her knowledge, engaged.

Mrs. Steuben turned her Southern eyes upon him with a look of almost romantic compassion. "To my knowledge? Why of course I'd know! I should think you'd know too. Didn't you know she was engaged? Why she has been engaged since she was sixteen."

Count Otto gazed at the dome of the Capitol. "To a gentleman from Utica?

"Yes, a native of her place. She's expecting him soon."

"I'm so very glad to hear it," said Vogelstein, who decidedly, for his career, had promise. "And is she going to marry him?"

"Why what do people fall in love with each other *for*? I presume they'll marry when she gets round to it. Ah if she had only been from the Sooth—!"

At this he broke quickly in: "But why have they never brought it off, as you say, in so many years?"

"Well, at first she was too young, and then she thought her family ought to see Europe—of course they could see it better *with* her—and they spent some time there. And then Mr. Bellamy had some business difficulties that made him feel as if he didn't want to marry just then. But he has given up business and I presume feels more free. Of course it's rather long, but all the while they've been engaged. It's a true, true love," said Mrs. Steuben, whose sound of the adjective was that of a feeble flute.

"Is his name Mr. Bellamy?" the Count asked with his haunting reminiscence. "D. F. Bellamy, so? And has he been in a store?"

"I don't know what kind of business it was: it was some kind of business in Utica. I think he had a branch in New York. He's one of the leading gentlemen of Utica and very highly educated. He's a good deal older than Miss Day. He's a very fine man—I presume a college man. He stands very high in Utica. I don't know why you look as if you doubted it."

Vogelstein assured Mrs. Steuben that he doubted nothing, and indeed what she told him was probably the more credible for seeming to him eminently strange. Bellamy had been the name of the gentleman who, a year and a half before, was to have met Pandora on the arrival of the German steamer; it was in Bellamy's name that she had addressed herself with such effusion to Bellamy's friend, the man in the straw hat who was about to fumble in her mother's old clothes. This was a fact that seemed to Count

Otto to finish the picture of her contradictions; it wanted at present no touch to be complete. Yet even as it hung there before him it continued to fascinate him, and he stared at it, detached from surrounding things and feeling a little as if he had been pitched out of an overturned vehicle, till the boat bumped against one of the outstanding piles of the wharf at which Mrs. Steuben's party was to disembark. There was some delay in getting the steamer adjusted to the dock, during which the passengers watched the process over its side and extracted what entertainment they might from the appearance of the various persons collected to receive it. There were darkies and loafers and hackmen, and also vague individuals, the loosest and blankest he had ever seen anywhere, with tufts on their chins, toothpicks in their mouths, hands in their pockets, rumination in their jaws and diamond pins in their shirt-fronts, who looked as if they had sauntered over from Pennsylvania Avenue to while away half an hour, forsaking for that interval their various slanting postures in the porticoes of the hotels and the doorways of the saloons.

"Oh I'm so glad! How sweet of you to come down!" It was a voice close to Count Otto's shoulder that spoke these words, and he had no need to turn to see from whom it proceeded. It had been in his ears the greater part of the day, though, as he now perceived, without the fullest richness of expression of which it was capable. Still less was he obliged to turn to discover to whom it was addressed, for the few simple words I have quoted had been flung across the narrowing interval of water, and a gentleman who had stepped to the edge of the dock without our young man's observing him tossed back an immediate reply.

"I got here by the three o'clock train. They told me in K Street where you were, and I thought I'd come down and meet you."

"Charming attention!" said Pandora Day with the laugh that seemed always to invite the whole of any company to partake in it; though for some moments after this she and her interlocutor appeared to continue the conversation only with their eyes. Meanwhile Vogelstein's also were not idle. He looked at her visitor from head to foot, and he was aware that she was quite unconscious of his own proximity. The gentleman before him

57

was tall, good-looking, well-dressed; evidently he would stand well not only at Utica, but, judging from the way he had planted himself on the dock, in any position that circumstances might compel him to take up. He was about forty years old; he had a black moustache and he seemed to look at the world over some counter-like expanse on which he invited it all warily and pleasantly to put down first its idea of the terms of a transaction. He waved a gloved hand at Pandora as if, when she exclaimed "Gracious, ain't they long!" to urge her to be patient. She was patient several seconds and then asked him if he had any news. He looked at her briefly, in silence, smiling, after which he drew from his pocket a large letter with an official-looking seal and shook it jocosely above his head. This was discreetly, covertly done. No one but our young man appeared aware of how much was taking place—and poor Count Otto mainly felt it in the air. The boat was touching the wharf and the space between the pair inconsiderable.

"Department of State?" Pandora very prettily and soundlessly mouthed across at him.

"That's what they call it."

"Well, what country?"

"What's your opinion of the Dutch?" the gentleman asked for answer.

"Oh gracious!" cried Pandora.

"Well, are you going to wait for the return trip?" said the gentleman.

Our silent sufferer turned away, and presently Mrs. Steuben and her companion disembarked together. When this lady entered a carriage with Miss Day the gentleman who had spoken to the girl followed them; the others scattered, and Vogelstein, declining with thanks a "lift" from Mrs. Bonnycastle, walked home alone and in some intensity of meditation. Two days later he saw in a newspaper an announcement that the President had offered the post of Minister to Holland to Mr. D. F. Bellamy of Utica; and in the course of a month he heard from Mrs. Steuben that Pandora, a thousand other duties performed, had finally "got round" to the altar of her own nuptials. He communicated this news to Mrs. Bonnycastle, who had not

58

heard it but who, shrieking at the queer face he showed her, met it with the remark that there was now ground for a new induction as to the self-made girl.

# About Author

**Henry James** OM (15 April 1843 – 28 February 1916) was an American-British author regarded as a key transitional figure between literary realism and literary modernism, and is considered by many to be among the greatest novelists in the English language. He was the son of Henry James Sr. and the brother of renowned philosopher and psychologist William James and diarist Alice James.

He is best known for a number of novels dealing with the social and marital interplay between émigré Americans, English people, and continental Europeans. Examples of such novels include The Portrait of a Lady, The Ambassadors, and The Wings of the Dove. His later works were increasingly experimental. In describing the internal states of mind and social dynamics of his characters, James often made use of a style in which ambiguous or contradictory motives and impressions were overlaid or juxtaposed in the discussion of a character's psyche. For their unique ambiguity, as well as for other aspects of their composition, his late works have been compared to impressionist painting.

His novella The Turn of the Screw has garnered a reputation as the most analysed and ambiguous ghost story in the English language and remains his most widely adapted work in other media. He also wrote a number of other highly regarded ghost stories and is considered one of the greatest masters of the field.

James published articles and books of criticism, travel, biography, autobiography, and plays. Born in the United States, James largely relocated to Europe as a young man and eventually settled in England, becoming a British subject in 1915, one year before his death. James was nominated for the Nobel Prize in Literature in 1911, 1912 and 1916.

## Life

### Early years, 1843–1883

James was born at 2 Washington Place in New York City on 15 April 1843. His parents were Mary Walsh and Henry James Sr. His father was intelligent and steadfastly congenial. He was a lecturer and philosopher who had inherited independent means from his father, an Albany banker and investor. Mary came from a wealthy family long settled in New York City. Her sister Katherine lived with her adult family for an extended period of time. Henry Jr. had three brothers, William, who was one year his senior, and younger brothers Wilkinson (Wilkie) and Robertson. His younger sister was Alice. Both of his parents were of Irish and Scottish descent.

The family first lived in Albany, at 70 N. Pearl St., and then moved to Fourteenth Street in New York City when James was still a young boy. His education was calculated by his father to expose him to many influences, primarily scientific and philosophical; it was described by Percy Lubbock, the editor of his selected letters, as "extraordinarily haphazard and promiscuous." James did not share the usual education in Latin and Greek classics. Between 1855 and 1860, the James' household traveled to London, Paris, Geneva, Boulogne-sur-Mer and Newport, Rhode Island, according to the father's current interests and publishing ventures, retreating to the United States when funds were low. Henry studied primarily with tutors and briefly attended schools while the family traveled in Europe. Their longest stays were in France, where Henry began to feel at home and became fluent in French. He was afflicted with a stutter, which seems to have manifested itself only when he spoke English; in French, he did not stutter.

In 1860 the family returned to Newport. There Henry became a friend of the painter John La Farge, who introduced him to French literature, and in particular, to Balzac. James later called Balzac his "greatest master," and said that he had learned more about the craft of fiction from him than from anyone else.

In the autumn of 1861 Henry received an injury, probably to his back, while fighting a fire. This injury, which resurfaced at times throughout his life, made him unfit for military service in the American Civil War.

In 1864 the James family moved to Boston, Massachusetts to be near William, who had enrolled first in the Lawrence Scientific School at Harvard and then in the medical school. In 1862 Henry attended Harvard Law School, but realised that he was not interested in studying law. He pursued his interest in literature and associated with authors and critics William Dean Howells and Charles Eliot Norton in Boston and Cambridge, formed lifelong friendships with Oliver Wendell Holmes Jr., the future Supreme Court Justice, and with James and Annie Fields, his first professional mentors.

His first published work was a review of a stage performance, "Miss Maggie Mitchell in Fanchon the Cricket," published in 1863. About a year later, A Tragedy of Error, his first short story, was published anonymously. James's first payment was for an appreciation of Sir Walter Scott's novels, written for the North American Review. He wrote fiction and non-fiction pieces for The Nation and Atlantic Monthly, where Fields was editor. In 1871 he published his first novel, Watch and Ward, in serial form in the Atlantic Monthly. The novel was later published in book form in 1878.

During a 14-month trip through Europe in 1869–70 he met Ruskin, Dickens, Matthew Arnold, William Morris, and George Eliot. Rome impressed him profoundly. "Here I am then in the Eternal City," he wrote to his brother William. "At last—for the first time—I live!" He attempted to support himself as a freelance writer in Rome, then secured a position as Paris correspondent for the New York Tribune, through the influence of its editor John Hay. When these efforts failed he returned to New York City. During 1874 and 1875 he published Transatlantic Sketches, A Passionate Pilgrim, and Roderick Hudson. During this early period in his career he was influenced by Nathaniel Hawthorne.

In 1869 he settled in London. There he established relationships with Macmillan and other publishers, who paid for serial installments that they would later publish in book form. The audience for these serialized novels was largely made up of middle-class women, and James struggled to fashion serious literary work within the strictures imposed by editors' and publishers' notions of what was suitable for young women to read. He lived in rented rooms but was able to join gentlemen's clubs that had libraries and where he could entertain male friends. He was introduced to English society by Henry Adams and Charles Milnes Gaskell, the latter introducing him to the Travellers' and the Reform Clubs.

In the fall of 1875 he moved to the Latin Quarter of Paris. Aside from two trips to America, he spent the next three decades—the rest of his life—in Europe. In Paris he met Zola, Alphonse Daudet, Maupassant, Turgenev, and others. He stayed in Paris only a year before moving to London.

In England he met the leading figures of politics and culture. He continued to be a prolific writer, producing The American (1877), The Europeans (1878), a revision of Watch and Ward (1878), French Poets and Novelists (1878), Hawthorne (1879), and several shorter works of fiction. In 1878 Daisy Miller established his fame on both sides of the Atlantic. It drew notice perhaps mostly because it depicted a woman whose behavior is outside the social norms of Europe. He also began his first masterpiece, The Portrait of a Lady, which would appear in 1881.

In 1877 he first visited Wenlock Abbey in Shropshire, home of his friend Charles Milnes Gaskell whom he had met through Henry Adams. He was much inspired by the darkly romantic Abbey and the surrounding countryside, which features in his essay Abbeys and Castles. In particular the gloomy monastic fishponds behind the Abbey are said to have inspired the lake in The Turn of the Screw.

While living in London, James continued to follow the careers of the "French realists", Émile Zola in particular. Their stylistic methods influenced his own work in the years to come. Hawthorne's influence on him faded during this period, replaced by George Eliot and Ivan Turgenev. 1879–1882 saw the publication of The Europeans, Washington Square, Confidence, and The Portrait of a Lady. He visited America in 1882–1883, then returned to London.

The period from 1881 to 1883 was marked by several losses. His mother died in 1881, followed by his father a few months later, and then by his brother Wilkie. Emerson, an old family friend, died in 1882. His friend Turgenev died in 1883.

## Middle years, 1884–1897

In 1884 James made another visit to Paris. There he met again with Zola, Daudet, and Goncourt. He had been following the careers of the French "realist" or "naturalist" writers, and was increasingly influenced by them. In 1886, he published The Bostonians and The Princess Casamassima, both influenced by the French writers he'd studied assiduously. Critical reaction and sales were poor. He wrote to Howells that the books had hurt his career rather than helped because they had "reduced the desire, and demand, for my productions to zero". During this time he became friends with Robert Louis Stevenson, John Singer Sargent, Edmund Gosse, George du Maurier, Paul Bourget, and Constance Fenimore Woolson. His third novel from the 1880s was The Tragic Muse. Although he was following the precepts of Zola in his novels of the '80s, their tone and attitude are closer to the fiction of Alphonse Daudet. The lack of critical and financial success for his novels during this period led him to try writing for the theatre. (His dramatic works and his experiences with theatre are discussed below.)

In the last quarter of 1889, he started translating "for pure and copious lucre" Port Tarascon, the third volume of Alphonse Daudet adventures of Tartarin de Tarascon. Serialized in Harper's Monthly Magazine from June 1890, this translation praised as "clever" by The Spectator was published in January 1891 by Sampson Low, Marston, Searle & Rivington.

After the stage failure of Guy Domville in 1895, James was near despair and thoughts of death plagued him. The years spent on dramatic works were not entirely a loss. As he moved into the last phase of his career he found ways to adapt dramatic techniques into the novel form.

In the late 1880s and throughout the 1890s James made several trips through Europe. He spent a long stay in Italy in 1887. In that year the short novel The Aspern Papers and The Reverberator were published.

### Late years, 1898–1916

In 1897–1898 he moved to Rye, Sussex, and wrote The Turn of the Screw. 1899–1900 saw the publication of The Awkward Age and The Sacred

65

Fount. During 1902–1904 he wrote The Ambassadors, The Wings of the Dove, and The Golden Bowl.

In 1904 he revisited America and lectured on Balzac. In 1906–1910 he published The American Scene and edited the "New York Edition", a 24-volume collection of his works. In 1910 his brother William died; Henry had just joined William from an unsuccessful search for relief in Europe on what then turned out to be his (Henry's) last visit to the United States (from summer 1910 to July 1911), and was near him, according to a letter he wrote, when he died.

In 1913 he wrote his autobiographies, A Small Boy and Others, and Notes of a Son and Brother. After the outbreak of the First World War in 1914 he did war work. In 1915 he became a British subject and was awarded the Order of Merit the following year. He died on 28 February 1916, in Chelsea, London. As he requested, his ashes were buried in Cambridge Cemetery in Massachusetts.

**Biographers**

James regularly rejected suggestions that he should marry, and after settling in London proclaimed himself "a bachelor". F. W. Dupee, in several volumes on the James family, originated the theory that he had been in love with his cousin Mary ("Minnie") Temple, but that a neurotic fear of sex kept him from admitting such affections: "James's invalidism ... was itself the symptom of some fear of or scruple against sexual love on his part." Dupee used an episode from James's memoir A Small Boy and Others, recounting a dream of a Napoleonic image in the Louvre, to exemplify James's romanticism about Europe, a Napoleonic fantasy into which he fled.

Dupee had not had access to the James family papers and worked principally from James's published memoir of his older brother, William, and the limited collection of letters edited by Percy Lubbock, heavily weighted toward James's last years. His account therefore moved directly from James's childhood, when he trailed after his older brother, to elderly invalidism. As more material became available to scholars, including the diaries of contemporaries and hundreds of affectionate and sometimes erotic letters written by James to younger men, the picture of neurotic celibacy gave way to a portrait of a closeted homosexual.

Between 1953 and 1972, Leon Edel authored a major five-volume biography of James, which accessed unpublished letters and documents after Edel gained the permission of James's family. Edel's portrayal of James included the suggestion he was celibate. It was a view first propounded by critic Saul Rosenzweig in 1943. In 1996 Sheldon M. Novick published Henry James: The Young Master, followed by Henry James: The Mature Master (2007). The first book "caused something of an uproar in Jamesian circles" as it challenged the previous received notion of celibacy, a once-familiar paradigm in biographies of homosexuals when direct evidence was non-existent. Novick also criticised Edel for following the discounted Freudian interpretation of homosexuality "as a kind of failure." The difference of opinion erupted in a series of exchanges between Edel and Novick which were published by the online magazine Slate, with the latter arguing that even the suggestion of celibacy went against James's own injunction "live!"—not "fantasize!"

A letter James wrote in old age to Hugh Walpole has been cited as an explicit statement of this. Walpole confessed to him of indulging in "high jinks", and James wrote a reply endorsing it: "We must know, as much as possible, in our beautiful art, yours & mine, what we are talking about — & the only way to know it is to have lived & loved & cursed & floundered & enjoyed & suffered — I don't think I regret a single 'excess' of my responsive youth".

The interpretation of James as living a less austere emotional life has been subsequently explored by other scholars. The often intense politics of Jamesian scholarship has also been the subject of studies. Author Colm Tóibín has said that Eve Kosofsky Sedgwick's Epistemology of the Closet made a landmark difference to Jamesian scholarship by arguing that he be read as a homosexual writer whose desire to keep his sexuality a secret shaped his layered style and dramatic artistry. According to Tóibín such a reading "removed James from the realm of dead white males who wrote about posh people. He became our contemporary."

James's letters to expatriate American sculptor Hendrik Christian Andersen have attracted particular attention. James met the 27-year-old Andersen in Rome in 1899, when James was 56, and wrote letters to Andersen that are intensely emotional: "I hold you, dearest boy, in my innermost love, & count on your feeling me—in every throb of your soul". In a letter of 6 May 1904, to his brother William, James referred to himself as "always your hopelessly celibate even though sexagenarian Henry". How accurate that description might have been is the subject of contention among James's biographers, but the letters to Andersen were occasionally quasi-erotic: "I put, my dear boy, my arm around you, & feel the pulsation, thereby, as it were, of our excellent future & your admirable endowment." To his homosexual friend Howard Sturgis, James could write: "I repeat, almost to indiscretion, that I could live with you. Meanwhile I can only try to live without you."

His numerous letters to the many young gay men among his close male friends are more forthcoming. In a letter to Howard Sturgis, following a long visit, James refers jocularly to their "happy little congress of two" and in letters to Hugh Walpole he pursues convoluted jokes and puns about their relationship, referring to himself as an elephant who "paws you oh so benevolently" and winds about Walpole his "well meaning old trunk". His letters to Walter Berry printed by the Black Sun Press have long been celebrated for their lightly veiled eroticism.

He corresponded in almost equally extravagant language with his many female friends, writing, for example, to fellow novelist Lucy Clifford: "Dearest Lucy! What shall I say? when I love you so very, very much, and see you nine times for once that I see Others! Therefore I think that—if you want it made clear to the meanest intelligence—I love you more than I love Others." To his New York friend Mary Cadwalader Jones: "Dearest Mary Cadwalader. I yearn over you, but I yearn in vain; & your long silence really breaks my heart, mystifies, depresses, almost alarms me, to the point even of making me wonder if poor unconscious & doting old Célimare [Jones's pet name for James] has 'done' anything, in some dark somnambulism of the spirit, which has ... given you a bad moment, or a wrong impression, or a 'colourable pretext' ... However these things may be, he loves you as tenderly as ever;

nothing, to the end of time, will ever detach him from you, & he remembers those Eleventh St. matutinal intimes hours, those telephonic matinées, as the most romantic of his life ..." His long friendship with American novelist Constance Fenimore Woolson, in whose house he lived for a number of weeks in Italy in 1887, and his shock and grief over her suicide in 1894, are discussed in detail in Edel's biography and play a central role in a study by Lyndall Gordon. (Edel conjectured that Woolson was in love with James and killed herself in part because of his coldness, but Woolson's biographers have objected to Edel's account.)

## Works

### Style and themes

James is one of the major figures of trans-Atlantic literature. His works frequently juxtapose characters from the Old World (Europe), embodying a feudal civilisation that is beautiful, often corrupt, and alluring, and from the New World (United States), where people are often brash, open, and assertive and embody the virtues—freedom and a more highly evolved moral character—of the new American society. James explores this clash of personalities and cultures, in stories of personal relationships in which power is exercised well or badly. His protagonists were often young American women facing oppression or abuse, and as his secretary Theodora Bosanquet remarked in her monograph Henry James at Work:

> When he walked out of the refuge of his study and into the world and looked around him, he saw a place of torment, where creatures of prey perpetually thrust their claws into the quivering flesh of doomed, defenseless children of light ... His novels are a repeated exposure of this wickedness, a reiterated and passionate plea for the fullest freedom of development, unimperiled by reckless and barbarous stupidity.

Critics have jokingly described three phases in the development of James's prose: "James I, James II, and The Old Pretender." He wrote short stories and plays. Finally, in his third and last period he returned to the long, serialised novel. Beginning in the second period, but most noticeably in the third, he increasingly abandoned direct statement in favour of frequent double negatives, and complex descriptive imagery. Single paragraphs began to run for page after page, in which an initial noun would be succeeded by pronouns surrounded by clouds of adjectives and prepositional clauses, far from their original referents, and verbs would be deferred and then preceded by a series of adverbs. The overall effect could be a vivid evocation of a scene as perceived by a sensitive observer. It has been debated whether this change of style was engendered by James's shifting from writing to dictating to a typist, a change made during the composition of What Maisie Knew.

In its intense focus on the consciousness of his major characters, James's later work foreshadows extensive developments in 20th century fiction. Indeed, he might have influenced stream-of-consciousness writers such as Virginia Woolf, who not only read some of his novels but also wrote essays about them. Both contemporary and modern readers have found the late style difficult and unnecessary; his friend Edith Wharton, who admired him greatly, said that there were passages in his work that were all but incomprehensible. James was harshly portrayed by H. G. Wells as a hippopotamus laboriously attempting to pick up a pea that had got into a corner of its cage. The "late James" style was ably parodied by Max Beerbohm in "The Mote in the Middle Distance".

More important for his work overall may have been his position as an expatriate, and in other ways an outsider, living in Europe. While he came from middle-class and provincial beginnings (seen from the perspective of European polite society) he worked very hard to gain access to all levels of society, and the settings of his fiction range from working class to aristocratic, and often describe the efforts of middle-class Americans to make their way in European capitals. He confessed he got some of his best story ideas from gossip at the dinner table or at country house weekends. He worked for a living, however, and lacked the experiences of select schools, university, and army service, the common bonds of masculine society. He was furthermore a man whose tastes and interests were, according to the prevailing standards of Victorian era Anglo-American culture, rather feminine, and who was shadowed by the cloud of prejudice that then and later accompanied suspicions of his homosexuality. Edmund Wilson famously compared James's objectivity to Shakespeare's:

One would be in a position to appreciate James better if one compared him with the dramatists of the seventeenth century—Racine and Molière, whom he resembles in form as well as in point of view, and even Shakespeare, when allowances are made for the most extreme differences in subject and form. These poets are not, like Dickens and Hardy, writers of melodrama—either humorous or pessimistic, nor secretaries of society like Balzac, nor prophets like Tolstoy: they are occupied simply with the presentation of conflicts of moral character, which they do not concern themselves about softening or averting. They do not indict society for these situations: they regard them as universal and inevitable. They do not even blame God for allowing them: they accept them as the conditions of life.

It is also possible to see many of James's stories as psychological thought-experiments. In his preface to the New York edition of The American he describes the development of the story in his mind as exactly such: the "situation" of an American, "some robust but insidiously beguiled and betrayed, some cruelly wronged, compatriot..." with the focus of the story being on the response of this wronged man. The Portrait of a Lady may be an experiment to see what happens when an idealistic young woman suddenly becomes very rich. In many of his tales, characters seem to exemplify alternative futures and possibilities, as most markedly in "The Jolly Corner", in which the protagonist and a ghost-doppelganger live alternative American and European lives; and in others, like The Ambassadors, an older James seems fondly to regard his own younger self facing a crucial moment.

**Major novels**

The first period of James's fiction, usually considered to have culminated in The Portrait of a Lady, concentrated on the contrast between Europe and America. The style of these novels is generally straightforward and, though personally characteristic, well within the norms of 19th-century fiction. Roderick Hudson (1875) is a Künstlerroman that traces the development of the title character, an extremely talented sculptor. Although the book shows some signs of immaturity—this was James's first serious attempt at a full-length novel—it has attracted favourable comment due to the vivid realisation of the three major characters: Roderick Hudson, superbly gifted but unstable and unreliable; Rowland Mallet, Roderick's limited but much more mature friend and patron; and Christina Light, one of James's most enchanting and maddening femmes fatales. The pair of Hudson and Mallet has been seen as representing the two sides of James's own nature: the wildly imaginative artist and the brooding conscientious mentor.

In The Portrait of a Lady (1881) James concluded the first phase of his career with a novel that remains his most popular piece of long fiction. The story is of a spirited young American woman, Isabel Archer, who "affronts her destiny" and finds it overwhelming. She inherits a large amount of money and subsequently becomes the victim of Machiavellian scheming by two American expatriates. The narrative is set mainly in Europe, especially in England and Italy. Generally regarded as the masterpiece of his early phase, The Portrait of a Lady is described as a psychological novel, exploring the minds of his characters, and almost a work of social science, exploring the differences between Europeans and Americans, the old and the new worlds.

The second period of James's career, which extends from the publication of The Portrait of a Lady through the end of the nineteenth century, features less popular novels including The Princess Casamassima, published serially in The Atlantic Monthly in 1885–1886, and The Bostonians, published serially in The Century Magazine during the same period. This period also featured James's celebrated Gothic novella, The Turn of the Screw.

The third period of James's career reached its most significant achievement in three novels published just around the start of the 20th century: The Wings of the Dove (1902), The Ambassadors (1903), and The Golden Bowl (1904). Critic F. O. Matthiessen called this "trilogy" James's major phase, and these novels have certainly received intense critical study. It was the second-written of the books, The Wings of the Dove (1902) that was the first published because it attracted no serialization. This novel tells the story of Milly Theale, an American heiress stricken with a serious disease, and her impact on the people around her. Some of these people befriend Milly with honourable motives, while others are more self-interested. James stated in his autobiographical books that Milly was based on Minny Temple, his beloved cousin who died at an early age of tuberculosis. He said that he attempted in the novel to wrap her memory in the "beauty and dignity of art".

**Shorter narratives**

James was particularly interested in what he called the "beautiful and blest nouvelle", or the longer form of short narrative. Still, he produced a number of very short stories in which he achieved notable compression of sometimes complex subjects. The following narratives are representative of James's achievement in the shorter forms of fiction.

- "A Tragedy of Error" (1864), short story

- "The Story of a Year" (1865), short story

- A Passionate Pilgrim (1871), novella

- Madame de Mauves (1874), novella

- Daisy Miller (1878), novella

- The Aspern Papers (1888), novella

- The Lesson of the Master (1888), novella

- The Pupil (1891), short story

- "The Figure in the Carpet" (1896), short story

- The Beast in the Jungle (1903), novella

- An International Episode (1878)

- Picture and Text

- Four Meetings (1885)

- A London Life, and Other Tales (1889)

- The Spoils of Poynton (1896)

- Embarrassments (1896)

- The Two Magics: The Turn of the Screw, Covering End (1898)

- A Little Tour of France (1900)

- The Sacred Fount (1901)

- Views and Reviews (1908)

- The Wings of the Dove, Volume I (1902)

- The Wings of the Dove, Volume II (1909)

- The Finer Grain (1910)

- The Outcry (1911)

- Lady Barbarina: The Siege of London, An International Episode and Other Tales (1922)

- The Birthplace (1922)

**Plays**

At several points in his career James wrote plays, beginning with one-act plays written for periodicals in 1869 and 1871 and a dramatisation of his popular novella Daisy Miller in 1882. From 1890 to 1892, having received a bequest that freed him from magazine publication, he made a strenuous effort to succeed on the London stage, writing a half-dozen plays of which only one, a dramatisation of his novel The American, was produced. This play was performed for several years by a touring repertory company and had a respectable run in London, but did not earn very much money for James. His other plays written at this time were not produced.

In 1893, however, he responded to a request from actor-manager George Alexander for a serious play for the opening of his renovated St. James's Theatre, and wrote a long drama, Guy Domville, which Alexander produced. There was a noisy uproar on the opening night, 5 January 1895, with hissing from the gallery when James took his bow after the final curtain, and the author was upset. The play received moderately good reviews and had a modest run of four weeks before being taken off to make way for Oscar Wilde's The Importance of Being Earnest, which Alexander thought would have better prospects for the coming season.

After the stresses and disappointment of these efforts James insisted that he would write no more for the theatre, but within weeks had agreed to write a curtain-raiser for Ellen Terry. This became the one-act "Summersoft", which he later rewrote into a short story, "Covering End", and then expanded into a full-length play, The High Bid, which had a brief run in London in 1907, when James made another concerted effort to write for the stage. He wrote three new plays, two of which were in production when the death of Edward VII on 6 May 1910 plunged London into mourning and theatres closed. Discouraged by failing health and the stresses of theatrical work, James did not renew his efforts in the theatre, but recycled his plays as successful novels. The Outcry was a best-seller in the United States when it was published in 1911. During the years 1890–1893 when he was most engaged with the theatre, James wrote a good deal of theatrical criticism and assisted Elizabeth Robins and others in translating and producing Henrik Ibsen for the first time in London.

Leon Edel argued in his psychoanalytic biography that James was traumatised by the opening night uproar that greeted Guy Domville, and that it plunged him into a prolonged depression. The successful later novels, in Edel's view, were the result of a kind of self-analysis, expressed in fiction, which partly freed him from his fears. Other biographers and scholars have not accepted this account, however; the more common view being that of F.O. Matthiessen, who wrote: "Instead of being crushed by the collapse of his hopes [for the theatre]... he felt a resurgence of new energy."

### Non-fiction

Beyond his fiction, James was one of the more important literary critics in the history of the novel. In his classic essay The Art of Fiction (1884), he argued against rigid prescriptions on the novelist's choice of subject and method of treatment. He maintained that the widest possible freedom in content and approach would help ensure narrative fiction's continued vitality.

James wrote many valuable critical articles on other novelists; typical is his book-length study of Nathaniel Hawthorne, which has been the subject of critical debate. Richard Brodhead has suggested that the study was emblematic of James's struggle with Hawthorne's influence, and constituted an effort to place the elder writer "at a disadvantage." Gordon Fraser, meanwhile, has suggested that the study was part of a more commercial effort by James to introduce himself to British readers as Hawthorne's natural successor.

When James assembled the New York Edition of his fiction in his final years, he wrote a series of prefaces that subjected his own work to searching, occasionally harsh criticism.

At 22 James wrote The Noble School of Fiction for The Nation's first issue in 1865. He would write, in all, over 200 essays and book, art, and theatre reviews for the magazine.

For most of his life James harboured ambitions for success as a playwright. He converted his novel The American into a play that enjoyed modest returns in the early 1890s. In all he wrote about a dozen plays, most of which went unproduced. His costume drama Guy Domville failed disastrously on its opening night in 1895. James then largely abandoned his efforts to conquer the stage and returned to his fiction. In his Notebooks he maintained that his theatrical experiment benefited his novels and tales by helping him dramatise his characters' thoughts and emotions. James produced a small but valuable amount of theatrical criticism, including perceptive appreciations of Henrik Ibsen.

With his wide-ranging artistic interests, James occasionally wrote on the visual arts. Perhaps his most valuable contribution was his favourable assessment of fellow expatriate John Singer Sargent, a painter whose critical status has improved markedly in recent decades. James also wrote sometimes charming, sometimes brooding articles about various places he visited and lived in. His most famous books of travel writing include Italian Hours (an example of the charming approach) and The American Scene (most definitely on the brooding side).

James was one of the great letter-writers of any era. More than ten thousand of his personal letters are extant, and over three thousand have been published in a large number of collections. A complete edition of James's letters began publication in 2006, edited by Pierre Walker and Greg Zacharias. As of 2014, eight volumes have been published, covering the period from 1855 to 1880. James's correspondents included celebrated contemporaries like Robert Louis Stevenson, Edith Wharton and Joseph Conrad, along with many others in his wide circle of friends and acquaintances. The letters range from the "mere twaddle of graciousness" to serious discussions of artistic, social and personal issues.

Very late in life James began a series of autobiographical works: A Small Boy and Others, Notes of a Son and Brother, and the unfinished The Middle Years. These books portray the development of a classic observer who was passionately interested in artistic creation but was somewhat reticent about participating fully in the life around him.

### Reception

### Criticism, biographies and fictional treatments

James's work has remained steadily popular with the limited audience of educated readers to whom he spoke during his lifetime, and has remained firmly in the canon, but, after his death, some American critics, such as Van Wyck Brooks, expressed hostility towards James for his long expatriation and eventual naturalisation as a British subject. Other critics such as E. M. Forster complained about what they saw as James's squeamishness in the treatment of sex and other possibly controversial material, or dismissed his late style as difficult and obscure, relying heavily on extremely long sentences and excessively latinate language. Similarly Oscar Wilde criticised him for writing "fiction as if it were a painful duty". Vernon Parrington, composing a canon of American literature, condemned James for having cut himself off from America. Jorge Luis Borges wrote about him, "Despite the scruples and delicate complexities of James, his work suffers from a major defect: the absence of life." And Virginia Woolf, writing to Lytton Strachey, asked, "Please tell me what you find in Henry James. ... we have his works here, and

I read, and I can't find anything but faintly tinged rose water, urbane and sleek, but vulgar and pale as Walter Lamb. Is there really any sense in it?" The novelist W. Somerset Maugham wrote, "He did not know the English as an Englishman instinctively knows them and so his English characters never to my mind quite ring true," and argued "The great novelists, even in seclusion, have lived life passionately. Henry James was content to observe it from a window." Maugham nevertheless wrote, "The fact remains that those last novels of his, notwithstanding their unreality, make all other novels, except the very best, unreadable." Colm Tóibín observed that James "never really wrote about the English very well. His English characters don't work for me."

Despite these criticisms, James is now valued for his psychological and moral realism, his masterful creation of character, his low-key but playful humour, and his assured command of the language. In his 1983 book, The Novels of Henry James, Edward Wagenknecht offers an assessment that echoes Theodora Bosanquet's:

> "To be completely great," Henry James wrote in an early review, "a work of art must lift up the heart," and his own novels do this to an outstanding degree ... More than sixty years after his death, the great novelist who sometimes professed to have no opinions stands foursquare in the great Christian humanistic and democratic tradition. The men and women who, at the height of World War II, raided the secondhand shops for his out-of-print books knew what they were about. For no writer ever raised a braver banner to which all who love freedom might adhere.

William Dean Howells saw James as a representative of a new realist school of literary art which broke with the English romantic tradition epitomised by the works of Charles Dickens and William Makepeace Thackeray. Howells wrote that realism found "its chief exemplar in Mr. James... A novelist he is not, after the old fashion, or after any fashion but his own." F.R. Leavis championed Henry James as a novelist of "established pre-eminence" in The Great Tradition (1948), asserting that The Portrait of a Lady and The Bostonians were "the two most brilliant novels in the language." James is now prized as a master of point of view who moved literary fiction forward by insisting in showing, not telling, his stories to the reader. (Source: Wikipedia)

# NOTABLE WORKS

## NOVELS

Watch and Ward (1871)

Roderick Hudson (1875)

The American (1877)

The Europeans (1878)

Confidence (1879)

Washington Square (1880)

The Portrait of a Lady (1881)

The Bostonians (1886)

The Princess Casamassima (1886)

The Reverberator (1888)

The Tragic Muse (1890)

The Other House (1896)

The Spoils of Poynton (1897)

What Maisie Knew (1897)

The Awkward Age (1899)

The Sacred Fount (1901)

The Wings of the Dove (1902)

The Ambassadors (1903)

The Golden Bowl (1904)

The Whole Family (collaborative novel with eleven other authors, 1908)

The Outcry (1911)

The Ivory Tower (unfinished, published posthumously 1917)

The Sense of the Past (unfinished, published posthumously 1917)

## SHORT STORIES AND NOVELLAS

A Tragedy of Error (1864)

The Story of a Year (1865)

A Landscape Painter (1866)

A Day of Days (1866)

My Friend Bingham (1867)

Poor Richard (1867)

The Story of a Masterpiece (1868)

A Most Extraordinary Case (1868)

A Problem (1868)

De Grey: A Romance (1868)

Osborne's Revenge (1868)

The Romance of Certain Old Clothes (1868)

A Light Man (1869)

Gabrielle de Bergerac (1869)

Travelling Companions (1870)

A Passionate Pilgrim (1871)

At Isella (1871)

Master Eustace (1871)

Guest's Confession (1872)

The Madonna of the Future (1873)

The Sweetheart of M. Briseux (1873)

The Last of the Valerii (1874)

Madame de Mauves (1874)

Adina (1874)

Professor Fargo (1874)

Eugene Pickering (1874)

Benvolio (1875)

Crawford's Consistency (1876)

The Ghostly Rental (1876)

Four Meetings (1877)

Rose-Agathe (1878, as Théodolinde)

Daisy Miller (1878)

Longstaff's Marriage (1878)

An International Episode (1878)

The Pension Beaurepas (1879)

A Diary of a Man of Fifty (1879)

A Bundle of Letters (1879)

The Point of View (1882)

The Siege of London (1883)

Impressions of a Cousin (1883)

Lady Barberina (1884)

Pandora (1884)

The Author of Beltraffio (1884)

Georgina's Reasons (1884)

A New England Winter (1884)

The Path of Duty (1884)

Mrs. Temperly (1887)

Louisa Pallant (1888)

The Aspern Papers (1888)

The Liar (1888)

The Modern Warning (1888, originally published as The Two Countries)

A London Life (1888)

The Patagonia (1888)

The Lesson of the Master (1888)

The Solution (1888)

The Pupil (1891)

Brooksmith (1891)

The Marriages (1891)

The Chaperon (1891)

Sir Edmund Orme (1891)

Nona Vincent (1892)

The Real Thing (1892)

The Private Life (1892)

Lord Beaupré (1892)

The Visits (1892)

Sir Dominick Ferrand (1892)

Greville Fane (1892)

Collaboration (1892)

Owen Wingrave (1892)

The Wheel of Time (1892)

The Middle Years (1893)

The Death of the Lion (1894)

The Coxon Fund (1894)

The Next Time (1895)

Glasses (1896)

The Altar of the Dead (1895)

The Figure in the Carpet (1896)

The Way It Came (1896, also published as The Friends of the Friends)

The Turn of the Screw (1898)

Covering End (1898)

In the Cage (1898)

John Delavoy (1898)

The Given Case (1898)

Europe (1899)

The Great Condition (1899)

The Real Right Thing (1899)

Paste (1899)

The Great Good Place (1900)

Maud-Evelyn (1900)

Miss Gunton of Poughkeepsie (1900)

The Tree of Knowledge (1900)

The Abasement of the Northmores (1900)

The Third Person (1900)

The Special Type (1900)

The Tone of Time (1900)

Broken Wings (1900)

The Two Faces (1900)

Mrs. Medwin (1901)

The Beldonald Holbein (1901)

The Story in It (1902)

Flickerbridge (1902)

The Birthplace (1903)

The Beast in the Jungle (1903)

The Papers (1903)

Fordham Castle (1904)

Julia Bride (1908)

The Jolly Corner (1908)

The Velvet Glove (1909)

Mora Montravers (1909)

Crapy Cornelia (1909)

The Bench of Desolation (1909)

A Round of Visits (1910)


**OTHER**


Transatlantic Sketches (1875)

French Poets and Novelists (1878)

Hawthorne (1879)

Portraits of Places (1883)

A Little Tour in France (1884)

Partial Portraits (1888)

Essays in London and Elsewhere (1893)

Picture and Text (1893)

Terminations (1893)

Theatricals (1894)

Theatricals: Second Series (1895)

Guy Domville (1895)

The Soft Side (1900)

William Wetmore Story and His Friends (1903)

The Better Sort (1903)

English Hours (1905)

The Question of our Speech; The Lesson of Balzac. Two Lectures (1905)

The American Scene (1907)

Views and Reviews (1908)

Italian Hours (1909)

A Small Boy and Others (1913)

Notes on Novelists (1914)

Notes of a Son and Brother (1914)

Within the Rim (1918)

Travelling Companions (1919)

Notebooks (various, published posthumously)

The Middle Years (unfinished, published posthumously 1917)

A Most Unholy Trade (1925, published posthumously)

The Art of the Novel : Critical Prefaces (1934)

CPSIA information can be obtained
at www.ICGtesting.com
Printed in the USA
LVHW042120191020
669187LV00016B/131

9 781662 718861